Making Mandi

SHYE RYDER

First Edition: October 2015

Publisher Mordant Media—A Division of Charlton Productions

Rogena Mitchell-Jones, Literary Editor
www.rogenamitchell.com

10 9 8 7 6 5 4 3 2 1

01

THE MOLTEN STEEL in the weld exploded. Tiny bits of white-hot shrapnel flew all over the leather-clad figure. Muffled by the large welding helmet, a stream of swearing reverberated. The pop continued to echo in the vast open space of the industrial loft.

The right hand lifted slightly and waited. The electronic sensor in the helmet shut off the small feed of electricity to the special glass, and the black mirror became clear. The deep brown eyes smoldered through the view. Amanda's eyes scanned over the weld as her mind raced through evaluations of starting over or to just flow more microwire into the hole and work it all out in the grinding.

The right hand eased forward and the fresh arc snapped into being—as searing as the noonday sun and just as damaging to the eyes. Half a millisecond after the arc started, the glass was the proper density of black. Amanda had hesitated to pay almost as much as her rent on a welding helmet. But the first time she didn't have to raise the face shield, she knew it had been a great investment.

Her right foot stepped on the feed pedal and the microwire of the welder flowed into and filled the hole. Amanda trailed out and started the rest of the weld. Stainless steel was a tricky weld, and it required every bit of her attention. The metal could overheat until the pocket exploded or run too fast and leave a snail track with no real weld.

The large buzzer at the door jarred the hulking leather clad woman. The weld exploded as she pushed the welding tip into the fluid steel—sending shrapnel flying about the space.

Her left hand whipped the helmet up and off as the right pulled the welding head away from any metal. "Cats fucking in the sunshine!" she blasted.

The buzzer growled again.

"Fuck," she muttered. She stood from the roll-around chair and turned, yelling, "I'm coming."

The temptation to grab the battered aluminum baseball bat that was leaning near the door was tempting. She glanced at the clock on the wall—quarter after seven. "Fuck."

Opening the door, she glared at Sam, her property owner and friend since the second grade.

"What?" Old friends were not exempt from Amanda's glare.

Sam teased with his bad imitation of gay talk and hand whiff. "Oh, gawd, girl—who put Ajax in your panties this morning? Because you are definitely sounding roughed up and ready to go."

She sagged against the door jam, trying hard not to be cheered by his humor. "Dial that fucking perky shit back about seventeen notches, creampuff. What do you want? I need to get to work." She started taking her leather welding jacket off by pulling on the snapped front Superman style.

Sam slapped his hands up to almost hide his eyes at the exposed tits. "Oh, gawd, girl. Stop that—my eyes are virgin." Amanda forgot she had not put a T-shirt on underneath.

Sam liked her breasts, but he had seen them at every stage of development. Nice as they were, they were not the size he liked. It had been a race to get his wife, Carol, and her double-Ds to the altar before Amanda took a crack at them. Occasionally, in the hot tub, the two girls still teased Sam by acting out one of his fantasies of girl on girl—but it never went farther than a little light petting and some sisterly peck kissing. Carol had known if she married Sam, she also got Amanda as part of the deal. The two were almost welded at the hip, where they both had matching tattoos of a puckered kiss—he on the right, she on the left.

Sam presented a small square envelope. "Your evil twin is getting married."

"I know. I threw the last one away."

"You had better read this one... I'm to be a groomsman, and you're a bridesmaid." He laid a finger on his chin and rolled his eyes. "Or was it the other way around?"

Amanda scowled. "Yeah, you'd look fucking cute in a pink frou-frou dress."

Deep in the bowels of the workshop, a large bell began to ring.

Amanda jumped. "Oh, shit. Now I really have to get to work."

Sam raised his hand as the door slammed. "Later," he said to the closed steel door.

As he turned, he glanced at his watch—7:31. He knew, almost to the minute, the back door would slam open and the large black motorcycle with a leathered rider would race out at 7:52. For anyone in a car, the race out to the computer campus would be a spin of the freeway roulette wheel. It could take twelve minutes or it could take an hour. Sam knew Amanda's commute would be somewhere between five and seven minutes. Splitting the lanes was illegal in Oregon, but he also knew the cops had to catch her before they could hand her a ticket.

True to form, the helmeted and all black leather figure strolled down the hallway. As she passed the security office, she did not even look—the right arm with a middle finger rose as she cruised past the open door. All of the security guards knew the sound of her boots. The custom installed steel ingots on the outer sides of her heels got just as much grinding time on winding roads as the dull clicking in the halls of the computer company. In the land of T-shirt to dress shirts with ties, nobody ever told the hot programmer that she was dressed inappropriately. Nobody dared. Nobody had ever heard of her pulling either of the knives that were set on each side of the tall boots, other than to see her slice an apple—but nobody wanted to.

If you asked anyone in the company if she had an attitude problem, they would all tell you that only if you were a computer chip that didn't work right. With people, she was either neutral or friendly. With her core fellow programmers that she felt were her equals, she was even playful.

The helmet came off, and she shook out her short self-hacked attempt at a pageboy haircut. The brown was an almost nice color, but the cut-by-kindergarten scissors was a perpetual train wreck that most people ignored and others thought she might have paid big bucks for that 'special' *I am dangerous* look. She placed the helmet on the shelf over the empty desk, kissed her two fingers, and then touched the date on the front. The numbers had white outspread wings.

She turned and walked three desks deeper into the cubical corral. The large Irish-Japanese-Samoan sat leaning back with his signature smile. She sat down on his lap as she draped her arm over his shoulders. Her fingers barely reached far enough to touch his far shoulder. Her arm pinned down the massive limb of a braid that she knew he was also sitting on, the tip of which might also be peeking out between his thighs—if there had been a separation between them.

"Good morning, sweetheart. How was the ride this morning?"

"Six minutes, forty-three seconds. Traffic was a bitch."

The man smiled. "Hmm, sounds like a mix of bad timing or you fucking just rolled a three. Those fucking trolls will get you in the back cavern and fuck you up."

Amanda had first met Samson at a D&D chat room. They had started exchanging ways to cheat on games that had moved from single-shooter to the cracked versions of Halo and Call of Duty. Both agreed the only way to play GTO was by the rules… and that was when he offered her a job. He only had to wait two years until she graduated from high school. He had been her mentor ever since. She had cracked her knuckles on cooled chipsets and connection speeds measured in MPSs. He had broken his on 8088s with dial-up.

"What have we got going, Obi-Wan?" They both scanned over the three 32-inch monitors.

He pointed at a set of figures. "You and Peter have been beating on this for two weeks now. I'm wondering if we have a sync problem that is deeper to the root…"

Amanda leaned in as she stripped off the leather jacket.

The black T-shirt had a worn neckline and a hole in the right sleeve. Samson knew the front at one time said *I didn't wake up with a bad attitude; don't make me go rent one*; it was the young woman's mantra toward life—and her only shirt that was not a plain white ribbed tank top.

He also knew this was Amanda, which meant zero ramp-up. She was already at full speed before the jacket came off—she would get her first of many cups of coffee later. It was why he hired her.

02

THE LARGE COFFEE in the cardboard heat wrapper was the only item on the desk that was incongruous. Every item was either utility or custom and special. The paperclips were standard, but they rested at the ready in a porcelain holder from Florence, Italy. The leather accessories were from Argentina or Spain, and the bud vase had been hand blown, while Victoria watched, in a tiny shop in Romania.

If one were to view her desk without knowing Victoria, they would think it was a prop for a movie; with everything laid out by measuring. Victoria's personal assistant would tell you that her boss merely put stuff down on the desk and expected it to find its exact place by itself. The truth was somewhere in between. Objects, people, appointments, and anything else in her life were not tolerated being out of where they should be in order to be efficient. Sloppiness was not what Victoria was paid $838,827.53 a year for—which did not include her benefits package, average performance bonuses, and partner profit sharing over the last three years.

Her perfectly manicured hand reached for the platinum

Monte Blanc pen that was a personal gift from the President of France. Each time she reached for it, she had a brief, fond memory of that evening in the Tour d'Argent. They had sat at a small table back away from the main gallery of the dining room. Their only neighbor was the floor to ceiling wall of windows overlooking the Seine. The president and his wife had graciously sat seated so that when the night settled, Victoria's view was the dark hulk of the backside of Notre Dame—until the lights came on to be timed with the arrival of dessert. They were celebrating her thirtieth as well as a successful outcome for a certain French company that was near and dear to their hearts—and personal portfolio.

Victoria looked over a couple of the expected reports on her desk and signed off on one. She glanced through the rest of the short stack.

She sipped at her coffee as she mulled over the short stack. Victoria shook a heft of blond curls out of her sight and glanced at her Patek Philippe watch. "Karen?"

Her assistant appeared in the open doorway a moment later. "Yes?"

Victoria read the last of the page and as she turned the page and brought the coffee back toward her lips, she mused. "I'm missing the brief on the Treadle, Krug, and Punket…"

"They called this morning and said there was new information important enough to vet and if accurate—to include in the brief. They were targeting right after lunch."

Victoria weighed the information as she looked at her assistant, but as Karen knew, she wasn't seeing her—it was the great whiteboard in her boss's head that Victoria was viewing.

"It's ten of eleven. Please call down and tell them that I

need it in my hands by a quarter of one so I can review and prepare for the three o'clock meeting." She looked back up at the turning woman. "And Karen…"

"Yes?"

"Make sure that whoever is doing the vetting is the one to deliver the brief. If there's more than one, I want them all here in case I have questions."

"Yes, Ms. Dumas."

"Oh, and Karen…"

The head appeared again.

Victoria picked up a hefty file, squared to the left corner of her desk. She made sure she had full eye contact with her assistant. Finally, she stood, still holding the file. She stepped from behind the desk and walked across the large office. Her assistant, feeling the weight of the action, moved back into the office.

Victoria waved her hand at one of the chairs by the desk as she sat at the other. Victoria thought back over the years that this woman had helped guide her through to the powerful position she was in today. Karen had been the seasoned mentor but without the title or acknowledgment. She had risen to head legal secretary at one of the largest firms in the Pacific Northwest. She might have moved higher, but age became her personal glass ceiling. A simple lunch was all it took Victoria to convince her to jump ship, take a small temporary cut in salary, but also be Victoria's personal assistant.

The older woman hesitated at the door.

"Please," Victoria pointed at the seat again.

The older woman put her hand on the door, looking askance. Victoria thought a moment and then nodded. Karen had shown the same kind of astute perception since the day

Victoria had poached her from the other firm. The woman had known that her career was stalled and saw the young, upstart lawyer as a way forward to a renewed interest, and a better position beyond the secretarial pool desk she had been sitting at for twelve years.

"Karen, I know you had the most to do with this report on the Leeper-Dunfield merger. I don't know who you pulled in for a team on it, but I want you to let accounting know. You and your team did an exceptional job on this."

"Thank you."

Victoria uncharacteristically extended her hand. "I knew the final on Friday, but I've been thinking about this all weekend long. I have informed accounting as to the bonus I would have received. It will pass to you and your team instead. I just wanted you to know how much I personally appreciate all that you do each day for the company and for me."

"It's the job—"

Victoria cut her off. "No, it's not. It is you, your work ethic, your knowledge and what you bring to my office personally, and the firm in general." She held up the file. "What you did with this, and what you have done since I hired you, goes way beyond the job description you signed on for. You never told me or anyone else that it was outside of your job—you just took it on, ran with it, and brought in a home run. I just thought it was time you knew your work and efforts have not gone unnoticed by the partners."

The older woman blushed slightly. "I appreciate you telling me, as well as the bonus."

Victoria thought a moment about the many hours the two of them worked side-by-side and had even shared lunches and dinners as they worked into the night. Yet Karen maintained her professional separation, even when Victoria had resorted to her first name.

Victoria sighed. "Karen, I know you have a lot more years of being professional than I have, but I think when it's just the two of us... Victoria instead of Ms. Dumas works for me just fine."

"Yes, Ms. Du... um, Victoria." She blushed faintly. "I'll work on it."

Victoria smiled softly and nodded as she put her hand on the older woman's shoulder. "Karen... about the bonus. I don't think you understand what we're truly talking about here. You are going to need to sit down with David on this— all of you. Your share is more than you made in the last five years combined. You need his help in looking at how this affects your financials. All of you are going to suffer a very large tax event, so the partners are here for all of you via David. His help is part of working here, so take advantage of his help. Normally he is not cheap. I know—he manages my portfolio."

"I don't know what to say."

Victoria grinned. "Just say thank you, because when you get your next paycheck, you're going to hate me. You'll never see your old tax bracket again, even with David's help. Your new compensation package is that of a full associate—which is something the partners think you have become, with or without a law degree."

Nervous, the older woman glanced at the large wall clock. "Oh, look at the time. Thank you again, but I need to get some work done."

Victoria nodded. "I have a few whips to crack myself." She noticed the welling of tears in the older woman's eyes, so she reached out and softly gripped the woman's hand. "I know these last several years your personal life hasn't been the best. However, you never walked through these doors with anything but a smile and cheer. Moving forward, I think things will be a lot better now. If you ever need to talk, I want you to know I live close, and we can talk. If there is anything, you need help with—we are family, and we try to take care of our family whenever we can. It might take some time to get used to it, but we're glad that you are part of our family."

The woman swallowed and cleared her throat. She spoke quietly. "Thank you… Victoria."

The two smiled and nodded as they stood. *A new understanding.*

03

THE MEETING PREDICTABLY ran a lot longer than the partners had originally speculated. The fresh information was about a problem that was no longer a possible financial irritation but had grown into not only a financial problem with catastrophic potential but some personal embarrassment for the management as well.

Victoria laid out the new information to the potential clients as well as the law firm's partners. The potential clients had hoped the firm would take them on before the problems had become general knowledge and the firm could not abandon them. At the outset, Victoria expressed, unequivocally, how much she advised the firm reject the clients. In the end, the new clients agreed to almost doubling the retainer for the first five years, as well as a moderate uptick on the billing for hours spent on the problem.

The clients and partners had spent the rest of the afternoon strategizing the path moving forward. One of their top partners would step down and retire early to spend time with his family—the one in Portland. The family he was maintaining in Los Angeles, as well as the mistress in Seattle, would be dealt with discretely.

Overall, the meeting and contract had worked out to the good. The work was not going to be easy over the next few years, but Victoria knew her staff would hammer out the details and make it all run like a Swiss watch.

With work over, Victoria retrieved her Lexus.

The short drive up into the Pearl District to buy a new outfit had not relieved Victoria's stress. She was very familiar with the fine natural fabric at the upscale boutique—especially silk.

She recognized she was getting knots in places she didn't get knots, and it affected her time on her daily runs. She was hoping a little get-away over the coming weekend would do the trick. Just her, open sand to run on, and the sea to swim in—no thinking about work or—

"Fuck."

Victoria froze in the dressing stall. The voice was guttural and bordered on male. She held the new dress up to her chest, clutching at the fabric for a sense of secured decency.

"What the fuck? How the hell do you get into this thing?"

Victoria relaxed a little. She could now tell the person talking was in the next stall and was female. Still clutching the dress to her silk bra, she looked up at the edge of the wall that separated the two changing booths. "Is there something you need help with?"

Her face heated at the returning silence. She realized how silly it was for her to look at the top of the booth when obviously nobody was tall enough to look over. She also realized she had not even started the conversation properly. After all, she did not even know who was on the other side.

"Hello? Is there something I could help with?" She was not even sure the other woman was still there. "My name is Victoria." She blushed. *How totally silly can I get? The woman would not care less who I am.*

The curtain swooshed back and Victoria jumped. She looked wide-eyed at the figure standing in front of her, dressed in a form-fitting tank top and white thong. In her hand was a summer dress.

"How the fuck am I supposed to put this on? The waist won't fit over my shoulders and it doesn't stretch."

Victoria stared at the hacked brown hair and deep brown eyes. The face had potential, but the hair was more than a bit scary. It looked hacked in chunks by something a gardener might use. The rest of the young woman was just amazingly toned—Victoria guessed a swimmer or body builder.

"Hello? Do you speak English?" Amanda stepped back and then looked in the third and last booth, which was empty. She came back to look at the obviously frightened woman in the second booth. "You *are* the woman that asked if she could help, aren't you?"

Victoria just nodded. She felt like a fool but didn't know what to say.

Amanda rolled her eyes and threw the dress over her shoulder and headed back to her changing booth. "Well, what the fuck. Seven words and we hit a brick wall of ignorance. I must have rolled a pair of shit dice this morning and didn't know it."

Victoria shook herself. She rushed out of the booth and followed Amanda to the other. "Wait... I'm sorry. I was... you just startled me, that's all."

Amanda turned on her and then relaxed. "Look, I'm

sorry. It's just been a long day from hell from start to finish, and all I want is to find a fucking dress, figure out how to put the damn thing on and go get a fucking beer." She sized up the woman standing in front of her. The blonde hair was layered in perfect fluffy, wavy curls and her clothes were tailored. Amanda guessed even the perfect bra was custom made. "I'm sure you have your own agenda of a wine bar with some hot stud from a high-rise or something. So if you'll just excuse—"

"Beer sounds good." Victoria surprised herself. "I mean... I don't drink beer, but it always sounded so... well... relaxed. It always sounded like a good time."

Amanda started to say something snide, and then just closed her mouth. This woman was making an effort. Obviously, they were from two very different worlds, but she was reaching out. Amanda took in the sheer silk bra with very fine and soft looking lace trim that lay perfectly flat on her smooth milky skin. The soft tan-pink was almost the color of her skin and gave the illusion of the larger breasts being nude. Amanda found the nude/not nude visual to be as much arousing as it was visually interesting.

Victoria carefully drew back a soft smile on her face. She shook her head of the long lazy curls that danced around her face and fell about her shoulders. She watched the other woman's eyes follow the movement and was slightly amused. "Now who's speechless?"

Victoria held out her hand. "Look, let's start over. Hi, my name is Victoria."

Amanda slumped and her left hand dropped with the dress in it. She shook. "Amanda. I'm sorry for... well, I'm just sorry. I know my way around welding, computers, and motorcycles." She held up the dress. "But this girl crap...

not so much."

Victoria hummed softly with a half-smile. "So you ride around on a motorcycle dressed in a little tight T-shirt and panties? How very… Portland. Do you ride nude, too?"

Amanda snorted with a crooked grin. "Not fucking like-ly."

They laughed together. Then there was an awkward moment.

Victoria broke it as she reached out for the dress. "Let's take a look at the torture suit." She smiled. The clothing that she thought nothing about was this woman's hell. She was also mindful that she might be just as useless trying to figure out those skintight leather outfits she saw some of the motorcyclist wearing around town.

She straightened the neckline and showed Amanda the hidden zipper. "It's designed to be as close to invisible as possible." She unzipped the dress. "Here, let me help you."

Without thinking, Victoria delicately took the bottom of Amanda's black tank-top and started to lift.

Amanda jumped back. "What are you doing?"

Victoria blinked. "Helping. You can't try on a sleeve-less dress with a T-shirt on—especially a black one. Even if it is a tank top." She laughed for almost three breaths… and then stopped. "Seriously? You've never worn dresses?"

Amanda growled with disgust. "Sixth-grade dance—I felt like a freak. I thought everyone could see my ass."

Victoria growled as she rested her hand on Amanda's shoulder. She nodded her head forward and looked through the tops of her eyes. "Everyone feels like a freak in the sixth grade. My mother thought boys were perverts, so she tried to get the rules changed so we girls could wear rompers instead of jumpers."

Amanda looked at her with a blank stare. "Wha…?"

"Think more like a shorts version of a bib-overall—that's the romper. The jumper is just a white shirt with a bib that hangs like a little cape."

Amanda snorted. "Like Fleet Week—the squids in their white Crackerjacks."

It was Victoria's turn to stare blankly. Then her mind sped up. "Ah, you mean the Navy and their uniforms." She smiled as Amanda nodded. "What did you call them?"

"Squids… if you ever went out with one, they seem to have eight arms."

Victoria closed one eye as she made the other large. "I never dated a gu… um, a Navy guy."

Amanda caught the slip, but let it go. She held up the dress. "So no shirt?"

"It would be for the best."

As Victoria blinked, the T-shirt disappeared. She had never seen a shirt removed in less than a half second. But then—she had never worn a T-shirt as an adult. She thought about how comfortable it might be… and liberating. As Amanda put the dress over her head, Victoria admired the firm chest. The breasts were at least a B, maybe a C, but there was nothing but tight firmness there. As Amanda moved, the muscles in her upper torso also rippled. Victoria thought about how it would feel to touch them. She wondered how hard the muscles were under that skin, how they would feel moving, maybe moving on top of…

"Bodybuilder." The word slipped out quietly with a sigh.

Amanda froze. "What?" The question was only slightly muffled from under the dress.

Victoria started pulling the dress down and arranging it

to fall into place. As Amanda's now even more misaligned hacked head of hair emerged, Victoria blushed slightly. "I said, with muscles like yours, you must spend a lot of time at the gym."

Amanda shook her head. "Never been—I don't have ti..." she saw herself in the mirror, "time." She studied the soft pastel floral pattern with the brown mop of hair sticking out. She started pulling frantically to take it off. "No fucking way. The twat twin can just go fuck themselves. This was a big fucking mistake from the start." The frantic movements became terror driven.

"Hey, calm down." Victoria tried to grab the panicked hands. "You're going to tear... You'll tear the dress... and have to pay... Stop it." She gave up and threw her arms around Amanda—trapping the flailing arms. "Would you just calm—" She could see the fear in Amanda's eyes.

Victoria waited out the panic. Finally, she felt the slump. Softly, she soothed. "Hey, it's okay. It's just us here. There is nothing wrong, nobody's making judgments." She smiled at Amanda with a crooked smile. "It's just a... it's just a fucking dress."

Amanda looked at her, and then a light went on in her eyes. She started to giggle. "You've never said *fuck* in your entire life, have you?"

Victoria tried to look offended. "Yes, I have. First year in college—I got a... I got a fucking B. I was really mad."

Amanda snorted and then started snickering. It was contagious, and Victoria was still hugging around Amanda's arms. Amanda's arms came up naturally to hang on.

As they softly laughed, their heads came close. Their faces came within an inch. They paused as they both realized where they were and that they knew nothing about the other.

They looked into each other's eyes, questioning. Both watched the other's curiosity and saw a need for acceptance—their eyes were mirrors of each other's fears and feelings.

Amanda closed the gap and softly landed on Victoria's narrow lips. She could smell the flowers in the soap Victoria used. Her lips opened just a tiny crack—hesitant trepidation. Amanda felt the gentle acceptance, and then a retreat. She could sense that she had maybe crossed a boundary. The other woman had stiffened. She stepped back.

She looked at the other woman. There was fear there. Victoria trembled ever so slightly. Amanda was scared she had just done something that couldn't be undone.

"I'm sorry. I didn't mean to..." She started pulling at the dress. Finally, she shimmied her shoulders out of the top and dropped it to the floor. With one foot, she kicked it into the corner of the dressing room. Victoria stood frozen as she watched Amanda fall apart and become defensive.

Amanda pulled on her leather pants and boots. She stood and tore the T-shirt onto her body and threw the leather jacket over her shoulder. Picking up the helmet, she stepped toward the woman in the doorway. "Excuse me. I'll be out of your life in a second."

Victoria stood her ground. She looked into the brown eyes. She saw the same pain that she herself knew all too well. She stepped into the other woman and crushed her lips on Amanda's in what she hoped would be felt as a passionate kiss. Her heart raced. She was in uncharted waters, but she knew she didn't want to be rescued.

Slowly, a stunned Amanda relaxed and put her arm around her. And she kissed her back. The kiss was dry, but there was feeling. Finally, Victoria withdrew with a couple of parting little bounce pecks. They opened their eyes and looked at each other in a calmer light.

Victoria started to speak and then cleared her throat. "That beer sounds really good right now."

Amanda thought about it for a few moments and then started laughing. "You've never had a beer in your life."

"I have too. Once…"

Amanda laughed. "Right after you said *fuck.*"

The two stood laughing until the shop dog came around the corner.

"Is everything okay? Is there anything I can get you?"

Victoria laughed. "No, we're fine. We got it all worked out. All we need now is a beer." She finished pulling her blouse on and buttoned the buttons, but only to almost decency.

"And a room," Amanda snorted.

The shop dog had a vacuous look on her frozen Northwest 23rd Avenue retail smile. "How did that dress work out?" Amanda could only picture the head flopping back and forth on shoulderpads as she asked *if they wanted fries with that.*

Victoria snorted, trying out her new word. "Oh, it was definitely fucked."

Amanda threw her arm around her new friend as they laughed and left, leaving the shop dog bewildered and smiling. She had not found the dress in the corner—yet.

04

THE DARK OF the bar would be the kind of place that Victoria's mother would have warned her about if her mother ever warned her of anything. Victoria remembered the little things—*hold hands when you cross the street*, and the favorite of all little girls, *be nice to people and they will be nice to you.*

She had been a lawyer long enough to know the rule was never applied once people grew up. She listened to the other partners in the firm who handled divorce and other family sports. One of the lawyers had asked if she wanted to go get a drink one night after work—she remembered his divorce was final a month before, and she knew just how ugly both sides had gotten. She told him she was prepping for a powerful meeting—something she was always doing. Anything but dating someone, she no longer had any respect for as a partner.

She followed the leather visage with the chopped hair as they wound their way through an almost empty dim-lit bar. She watched as the bartender looked up and Amanda gave him the peace sign. Then Victoria realized it was probably simpler just ordering two beers.

Victoria knew all of her warning bells should have been going off. If they were, they were doing it somewhere else. The low-hanging dark-wood ceiling made it seem like the kind of bar murder mysteries were written about. Victoria's alarms weren't going off as she followed what normally she would consider to be a scary looking person dressed in tight black leather, with what appeared to be—and probably were—knives sticking, somehow, out of her boots. Everything was warning Victoria to run the other way. Yet she found herself drawn toward this woman. Even if it meant following her into a dark and forbidding place.

Amanda approached a table for four, placed her helmet gently in the middle, and added a two-finger kiss. Pulling a chair around from the smaller table next to it, she sloughed out of the leather jacket and threw it over the back of one of the other chairs. She sat and slid into a slouch with malcontent.

Victoria drew out the chair on the other side of the table and sat. She looked across the roughly lit bar. The seating was mostly empty except for the few older men lining the bar. She wondered if this was a usual place for Amanda or just an occasional destination.

Victoria screwed her mouth up into a skewed smile. "Well, fuck—we're here." She looked over at Amanda, who was watching the men at the bar. Amanda started gently laughing.

Finally, Amanda sat up and leaned on the table as the bartender brought the beers. Amanda glanced up and just mouthed, *tab*. She took up one of the glasses and held it out. "Here's to your first legal drink of a real beer."

They clinked glasses, and Victoria took a sip as she watched over the rim of the glass. Amanda washed almost a third of the beer in one wave. The bitter yeasty taste hit Victoria, and she placed the glass on the table. She stared at the beer.

"It's not refined if that is what you were expecting. This is basic draft—probably PBR." Amanda took another swig, although smaller.

"PBR?"

"Probably." Amanda followed with a low, quiet rolling belch. "Yup, it's got that smooth Midwest fertilizer aftertaste." Then realizing that Victoria had no clue about the beer, she explained. "The beer is made in the Midwest somewhere."

Victoria giggled. "So, you burp to discover the aftertaste? I always wondered what that was for."

Amanda repeated a much smaller burp. "It works best with beer. Although there is a certain way to belch that is great for discovering where a steak was raised." She looked the other woman square in the eyes—challenging her to call her on the bullshit.

Victoria stared back, accepting the challenge, but not sure where to take it. This wasn't the kind of in fighting the legal system prepared her for. "Sounds special, but I'm sure I don't eat that sort of steak. At least, not a steak which would require the need for such information."

Amanda leaned back in her chair and took a slow sip, watching the blonde.

"Are you always prim and proper or just on Tuesdays?" Amanda's voice was soft and level. Victoria could feel there was a certain snide touch, but it was masking the serious question.

"I try to be as nice as I would like to be treated. I take it that doesn't work for you in your world?"

Amanda flexed her eyebrows and half rolled her eyes. "Nah, it works. I just kind of forget to do it sometimes."

"You mentioned something about steel and computers and motorcycles. Did I remember that right?"

"I'm a digital dork by day and trying to be a metal sculptor at night. Unless I'm out getting a beer with a friend."

Victoria almost asked about the friend but was stuck on the day job. "Digital dork?"

"I hack code." She glanced over at the question mark on the other's face. "I'm a computer programmer." The face cleared.

"So you write the system code that makes computers run."

Amanda's mouth opened, and then she thought about her real job. To even most code writers, what she did was more like magical alchemy. She closed her mouth and nodded. "Yeah."

Victoria made her living at reading people. "Yeah—but not exactly. It's like me—I'm a lawyer, but I have rarely been in a courtroom."

Amanda eyed the untouched glass in front of the woman sitting properly at the table. "Kind of like drinking beer." She stood and walked toward the bar.

Victoria watched the leather-skinned hips as she swayed around the tables and chairs—every piece of furniture, missed by only two inches. The movements were like watching a pianist's hands during a concert. Poetry in motion—except she hadn't realized the music had stopped playing when she reached the bar—her eyes were fixed on the area where the white tank-top ended and the leather tucked in… in interesting ways.

"Hey, Jeff, do you have any Thai beer? Something more to the taste of a wine drinker?"

The bearded man smiled and leaned down to the cooler. Drawing out a Singha, he popped the cap and pulled a frozen glass from the freezer. "Dating upscale these days?"

Amanda snorted. "No date, dude. I kissed her in the dressing room, and I think her hand reached for her Bible." She glanced over her shoulder. "Dude, I don't know what I'm doing here. I offered a beer, and I think she's just curious."

The man shrugged. *To each their own.*

Amanda walked back as she poured the beer into the glass. She offered it out. "Here, try this instead."

Victoria took a sip, and then another. "That's very different." She took the bottle in her other hand and examined the label.

Amanda took the draft and sat down next to her empty glass. "It's imported from Thailand. PBR is made here."

The woman set the bottle and glass down after another sip. "It tastes like liquid satin." She looked at Amanda. "What's PBR?"

Amanda snorted. "PBR stands for Pro Bull-riding Rodeo, unless we're talking beer—then it's Pabst Blue Ribbon. There are over a hundred micro brews made in Portland alone. But gallon for gallon, PBR is over sixty percent of all beer sold in Portland."

Victoria frowned as she took another sip of her beer. "Why so much?"

"Because it's cheap. Taste is king, but the almighty buck wins the day."

Amanda drained the other glass and stood. "Look, stay and enjoy your beer, but I need to get some welding done tonight." She stuck her hand out. "It was nice meeting you and all…"

Victoria grabbed her purse and stood as she opened it, ignoring the extended hand. "Let me get this."

"It's on my tab."

"At least let me take care of the tip."

"Suit yourself."

Victoria took a ten from her purse. She knew it was a large tip but wasn't going to ask what a standard tip was in a place like this. "I'll walk you out." She looked up with a horrified look on her face. "I mean, I'll walk out with you."

Amanda leaned over and gently took up her helmet with both hands. "Chill," She turned. "I knew what you meant."

As they stepped out of the door onto the sidewalk, Amanda sought to make amends. "Look, I'm sorry about that back in the dressing room."

They came to a stop next to the black motorcycle.

"It's okay. I've seen people lose it before when they're in uncharted territory, like that dress."

"No, I meant about kissing you and all. I misread—"

"It's all right. Really. I was just… unprepared."

"Scared is more like it." Amanda chuckled softly.

"Some… but I think I—" Victoria suddenly leaned over and kissed Amanda. Amanda stiffened and then relaxed. They parted. "Yes. I think I liked it."

Amanda stepped closer and eased her free hand around Victoria's waist. Their mouths were only an inch apart. Amanda could feel the other woman's breath shorten and increase. The smell of her soap again filled her nose with a flowery citrus scent—spring in an orange orchard.

Victoria leaned in as her mouth opened slightly. Their tongues met as the lips touched. Someone gave out a small moan. There was a hesitant examination. Tongues ran along lips and the edging of teeth. The heat of the hand on Victoria's back became like a candle held close.

A noise from across the street and the moment was broken. Victoria stepped back, embarrassed by where she was and doing what people usually did behind closed doors.

Amanda realized what was going through the other's mind. "Relax, nobody saw your privates. This is Portland—women kiss all the time on the street."

Strictly by reflex, Victoria justified herself. "But I'm not one of those wo—" She cut herself off as she realized she was talking to *one of those kinds of women—that she had just kissed on the street.* She blushed in horror, turned, and rushed off.

Amanda stared. She tried to figure out what just happened, but the gears in her mind were mud or slush. Nothing was processing. The fourth woman she had ever seriously kissed in her life had just basically told her that she was straight, and Amanda was one of *those* women, and the two were mutually exclusive.

"Fuck."

05

THE WELDING WAS shaky and the large puddle of molten steel popped. One of the tiny missiles of white hot metal found the smallest of cracks between the helmet and the neck of the jacket.

Amanda jumped up. "Fuck me blind!" She pushed the helmet up and ripped open the jacket. With her gloved hand, she slapped at the tiny painful burn. "Crap! That hurts!"

She reached over with the toe of her boot and flicked the big switch off. The silence did not help. Removing the helmet, she looked at the face formed in steel. The lips were still not right. The upper lip just hung from the nose. The indent was a smooth 'V' dent, but the lips themselves were lifeless. She was at a loss for how to fix it.

She looked over her shoulder at the clock. *Damn.*

As she strode toward the area that was her bathroom, she shed leather. Jacket fell behind, apron to the left, her left toe rode the right heel and she stepped out of the boot. Hopping, she slid the left off and it flew over her shoulder toward its mate. Magnets, hidden in the leather of each sheath, kept the two knives in place. Thumbs and forefingers winged open the snap on her pants, and the zipper had barely hit bottom when the fingers slid down the sides of the legs as she bent forward. She stepped out of the pile of leather, catching her cotton thong with her right toe and flipped it at the corner, which was the hamper. Nothing was there but white thongs, white socks, white tank tops and the occasional white sports bra—a pile of utility white. She had worn boxers when she was young and into jeans, but they bunched up under the snug-fitting leather. Amanda was all about what worked, was the least complicated, and was comfortable—just like the layout of the industrial loft that was her home, workspace, and garage. The tank top hit the wall and dropped to the pile.

The water ran toward warm as she brushed her teeth—*forty-eight strokes on each quadrant—thirty-six on the smaller inside*. She smiled at the mirror. *At least I have a decent set of teeth*. She sidestepped into the area of tile that was the shower. Everything in the industrial space was open. The bed was up against the wall so she could lean and read at night. One of her former lovers had gone nuts that Amanda could watch her as she peed, pooped, wiped, or took a shower. Much like Amanda, and how she lived her life, everything was in the open. As she rinsed her hair and wrung it dry, she thought about how different she was from that secretive baby dyke that she had brought home for a couple of attempts at a relationship. The girl was afraid of her own shadow, not to mention her sexuality. She had discovered she was a lesbian but was not sure what that really meant or what to do. She was a complete one-eighty degrees from Amanda—and how Amanda had grown up.

Amanda had come to breakfast one day as a thirteen-year-old. She had thought long and hard. She told her parents over pancakes with strawberry syrup that she wanted to have a girlfriend. They had nodded as parents do at that age. *Of course, you want to have a friend.*

She then, between bites, explained that she wanted to kiss and sleep with and touch this girlfriend. The table had taken a chilled turn. Her twin was confused. She had always been her friend—they had always been inseparable.

Her father cleared his throat and asked if she had anyone specific in mind. She did.

But as it turned out, the girl was madly in love with the new kid who had just made the junior varsity football team. Amanda moved on.

Soon, she had been in more fights than she had been kissed. Two years later, she found a couple of friends. Jeff had been there all along, but Amanda just had not seen him standing there. Jeff had his own fights. They ended high school holding hands and walking arms around each other. The hugs were there—but just as friends. He was still looking for a boyfriend—or at least a nice girl who would let him have a guy on the side. It had always been complicated with him.

The other friend was even closer to home and would always be there. Jody was part of her family. She and her brother, Sam, had become part of their family when Amanda and Sam were in the second grade. Jody was a few years older but had been intrigued by Amanda's statement. Soon, she became her friend, lover, mentor, and all-around partner.

Amanda stood under the flow of the large showerhead called a sunflower. It was more of a flood of water than what a usual shower head gave off. Amanda knew the difference; the regular low-flow showerhead was four feet down the wall. But, tonight called for the speed of the flood—she was already late, and the Master would have her in a corner if she ruined the game.

She glanced across the openness of the room to the oversized clock that was above the metal sculpture. Amanda realized she had been standing under the waterfall of hot water far longer than she should have or had wanted.

It was the lips... they were bothering her. Why could she not make them the way she wanted? The lips on her sculpture were lifeless—but then, so was steel. But, in her mind, she knew she could make them...

Ignoring her wet hair, she pulled on her leathers, grabbed her small D&D backpack and hit the switch for the door as she pulled on her helmet. Turning the key, she hit the starter and kicked the bike into gear. She let out the clutch and shot down the small alley. The alley was a dead-end that ran only to her door. The Radio Frequency Identification chip in her helmet closed the roll-down door as she roared past the doorway checkpoint. The checkpoint sensor three-quarters of the way down the alley triggered the alarm system. Upon her return, the sensor would know the alarm was on and the door was down—so it would cancel the alarm and open the door. As long as Amanda was not going faster than seventeen miles per hour, the door would be open when she got to it. As she passed the door sensor, it would begin closing the door. It was the closest to the Bat Cave the nerd in her would go.

The Portland evening had only slightly cooled. She wound through the industrial buildings and leaned over as she turned up the street that during the day was lined with trucks backed into loading docks. The old V-Max could have hit well over a hundred by the time it reached the end of the long block, but she always settled for a short wheel walk on the back tire and then pulling into the open bay door about half-way down the block.

As she twerked the throttle, she realized why the lips on her sculpture were wrong. She stuttered and almost dropped the bike. She recovered and stopped. The sight down the industrial street with the old railroad tracks in the middle dissolved into the briefest of sights. The sunlight glanced across the upper edge of the thin lips. The groove, called the philtrum, on her upper lip, just under her thin nose was a tiny ski jump. The sunlight had delicately rimmed the Cupid's bow on the lip in nothing larger than a thin pencil line. It had stunned Amanda then and stopped her now.

"In fourteen seconds, I'm rolling this door down. You're either in or out."

The large Irish-Japanese-Samoan-Hawaiian stood with his hands on the chain. He was old school. Even his bathroom had walls. They were shoji screens, but they were walls. To play in his dungeon, you played by his rules—inside the old wooden warehouse, the interior was all polished wood and Japanese. The drink for tonight would be green tea, served traditionally by his wife. No beer. No saké. Tonight was all D&D.

Amanda kicked the bike into gear and pulled in under the closing door. She knew she had already broken his first rule of being on time.

She dismounted and removed her helmet. There was a special low table in the middle of the parking area with three motorcycles and four bicycles. The table was for Amanda's helmet. Nothing else was ever placed on it.

She turned and placed her hands together. She bowed low. "Sorry, Papa." There were no excuses other than him having to come get her out of jail or bring a lily to her hospital bed. There were results—or meaningless stories.

He bowed gracefully. "Leave your boots on. You are late as it is. You can apologize to Tosika later."

The game had started ten minutes late, but Samson was relentless, and at the stroke of ten, the game ended. By ten after the hour, the man rolled down the door as his wife rolled out the futon bed and what had been a parlor of nerds became their bedroom. His castle, his rules, but her home—the giant of a man worshiped the ground his wife walked on.

Amanda stopped at the main street. The image of the woman's lips haunted her. Instead of turning up and back into the industrial area, she turned left and motored the four blocks to the freeway entrance. The split approached in seconds, and she chose the left. As she rode up over the Fremont Bridge, she slowed and looked down the river that bisected the city of Portland. The lights on the water were a wash across the calm mirror. Amanda took that calm into her being as she looked down the river. It was deep and cool, and what seemed to be still, Amanda knew it was an optical illusion—it was racing along at five miles per hour, even in the summer.

She dropped the bike through the center to transition on to the I-5 north. As the curve dropped to the lower freeway, Amanda pushed the envelope. The needle was hovering at ninety as she backed off and dropped left into the center lane. There were few places she could really open up the old bike. In its day, the V-Max was the stunning powerhouse of the mid-sized bikes. With only forty-five cubic inches, it was considered small when placed against the seventy-four of the Harley. But from a dead stop, or a chance meeting on the freeway, the V-Max showed that the older, slower design was no match.

The old green bridge always appeared as a surprise. No matter how she watched for the main bridge that crossed from Oregon to Washington, she eased around a corner and dropped off from a slow rise, and there it stood before her. It was never a pretty bridge, it was just a classic. She loved riding fast in the slow lane so the wind sounded rippled by the uprights of the trestle bridge that was almost a hundred years old. At the end was a quick off-ramp that transitioned to the I-14 on the Washington side of the Columbia River.

Amanda squeezed on the power, and the bike leaned just right as she came out of the last curve with the needle over a hundred. If there were no red light or siren behind her in the next thirty seconds, she would hit the one-forty mark by the end of a mile. Nine miles or five minutes later, she dropped the speed back to sixty and held it there all the way back across the Glen Jackson Bridge. She rode in the breakdown lane so she could see over the retaining wall. The mighty Columbia River was wide and smooth. A few lights downriver were from fishermen dabbling around, probably fishing for trash fish. If anything like salmon or steelhead were running, you could walk across the river from boat to boat.

The air was calm and had finally cooled. The bike slid along the blacktop. Amanda's mind was aware of the other cars and the highway but was also stuck on the light along the lips.

The exit ramp onto the I-84 had come and gone before she remembered where she was going. She thought about just taking the grand loop down to where the 205 met up with the I-5 again, and backtrack to home, but she remembered she needed to be at work a bit early the next morning.

She squared the return by getting off at Stark Street, took it to 82nd Avenue, and ran back up to the I-84 and headed back into Portland and the industrial area. The air had cleared her mind, and the speed had fed her warrior soul. The tea that Tosika had served she knew would also cleanse her body. She thought about asking what kind it was—it would probably be better for her than having a PBR at Jeff's.

As she pulled into her home, she chuckled at the thought of teaching Jeff how to make a proper cup of tea and serving her at the bar. He would probably like the traditional kimono Tosika wore, but making something more complicated than a draft beer just was not Jeff's style.

06

THE DAY HAD been a mixed bag of shit and grits. With enough grits, you can eat the shit—but it's still just shitty grits. Amanda scratched at the left side of her chest and realized there was a hole in the shirt that she could stick her thumb through. It was on the side of the breast—not the nipple—but the other nerds had probably been getting off watching the naked skin move past it nonetheless.

She reached down into the bottom drawer for her spare white tank-top stash. She took the one off the top and snapped it out on the desk in front of her. She grabbed the armpit of the shirt on the left side with her right hand, and in one long fast arc, swept the shirt off. The holey shirt arched over the cubical wall into the next cubby as both of her hands dove into the fresh shirt, which slipped over her head.

As she reached down to pull the tight bottom of the shirt over her chest and tummy, the voice rumbled behind her, "Got a hot date tonight?"

She turned to look at Samson leaning back around the corner. His giant ponytail hung to the floor. His smile was more of amusement than lust. She slowly pulled the shirt down. She watched him the entire time. His eyes never left hers. Her breasts held no interest to him. She knew he only had eyes for his wife.

"I think I burned a hole in the…" she mumbled.

His smile grew as he held the shirt up with his middle finger poking through the hole. "I saw the hole earlier. It was posted on Nerd-Life.com."

"Shit." She hung her head. "Is nothing sacred anymore?"

"There was no attribe—but I hacked in and took it down anyway. It had only gotten seventy-five hits, but no shares or re-tweets."

"How long was it up?"

"About two hours."

"Two hours and only seventy-five hits?"

Samson started laughing. "Hundred. Seventy-five *hundred* hits—China and India were not awake yet. If they'd seen it, it would have been millions, and at least four hundred memes would've gone viral. You would've been more famous than Farrah Fawcett."

"Who?"

The smile left his face and he sat up. His chair disappeared back into his cubical. Amanda turned around to see what had caused his change. There was nobody there. The smile crept across her face. "It's okay, old man."

"Fuck you, kid."

The two quietly chuckled. Without looking, Amanda slapped the hand that was low at the cubical wall—palm up. *Well played.*

A few hours later, the 26 Freeway was stacked up and looked like the end of summer heat was making the drivers bitchy and crazy. Amanda opted out and headed for Cornell. She'd rather take the back roads than have some asshole in his Beemer open his door on her as she cut the lane. It wasn't legal, but she didn't want to hear some butthead try to quote the vehicle code to her when all she wanted was the cool dark of Jeff's bar and a skanky glass of beer.

Amanda rested the helmet on the bar. Jeff gently picked it up and placed it in an empty niche that was just the right size and kept it out of harm's way. Jeff cared about the helmet as much as Amanda did. His partner built the helmet, and then painted the image of the Cassiopeia cluster on the helmet. It was a labor of love and the last amazing art project Lane had done before he died of AIDS. Amanda knew Jeff also had it but was luckier that they had caught it early, and he controlled it with massive amounts of drugs. Everything that came in from the bar went to keeping Jeff alive.

Jeff put the glass of PBR down on a coaster and then laid a business card next to it.

"What's this?" Amanda took a sip as she looked at the card. The last name of the person was the third name in the firm's name. There were only four last names in the firm, but the last name of associates and the three-floor address in one of the best buildings in town caused Amanda to set the beer down slowly. "Holy crap... Did you look at this?"

"She didn't know how to get ahold of you, but she figured you might occasionally come in here, and I might know you. I think she wants another beer... but not with me." He smiled wanly. "She seemed a little... lost. Like she didn't know what she really wanted, but she wanted to still talk to you. Like you might have some answers."

"I don't think she knows what she wants. I don't think she's ever been laid—male or female."

Jeff stopped polishing the glass. "I seem to remember someone else like that."

She knew what he was referring to, but she wasn't going easy. "Yeah, but at least he finally found a nice guy."

Jeff kept polishing a beer glass as he gave Amanda a hard look and continued. "Of the large crowd here right now, I'm the only one who has ever been successful at having a loving relationship beyond renting a U-Haul in the same week. Relationships aren't like the ones you had with your folks and siblings. There's a lot of work that goes into reaching out and taking another strange hand. The path of discovery doesn't only run through the sheets on a bed or entail rug burns—it's about honest talking and sometimes just listening to another person's heart. Maybe you might have to get off that screaming eagle bike of yours and just take a quiet walk. If you truly find something—is that such a huge price to pay?"

Jeff put the glass in the freezer, threw the towel onto his shoulder, and leaned on the bar with both hands spread out so he could bring his face close. "Look, Amanda, don't be an asshole. You needed a friend the same time I needed one. So what—we got lucky. Maybe she has a big to-do job with a fancy address—so what? You think those kinds of people don't need someone who might help them just figure out the simple shit?"

He glared at her as she deadpanned him. "So you're some kind of hardass lesbian whose life is squared away. Big fucking whoop-dee-do. I remember you freaking out because your big-ass gaming machine had gone tits-up and was toast. I came over and the first thing I asked you was why it was unplugged."

"You're an asshole for bringing that up again. I was just

a kid."

He snorted angrily. "It was only four fucking years ago—grow the fuck up."

She smiled shyly. "It was five… but who's counting?"

"I am… so call her."

She stuck the card in her back pocket. "Okay, asshole… I'll call her. Give me another beer."

He stood up and grabbed another glass to polish. "You're cut off. Go home and create something. I want to see that face you've been working on."

"I've got a picture of it here." She pulled her phone out of her back pocket.

Jeff leaned in and laughed a sharp one-note laugh. "If you have even one picture on that phone, I will give you that beer for free."

They stared with their faces inches apart. "That's what I thought. No picture, but you just pulled that woman's card out of your back pocket and dumped it on my floor like a 23rd Street tease."

Amanda replayed where she had put the card, and where her phone was. She knew he was right. She stood up. "Give me my helmet, asshole."

"Pick up her card and show me that you put it in your wallet. *Then* I'll give you Lane's helmet."

She reached down, retrieved the card, and stuffed it in her wallet. As she stuffed the small wallet in her front pocket, he handed her the helmet.

As she took hold of it, he held on. "I love you, but I'm serious. You need to give this woman a chance—even if it means she turns out to be a friend instead of a lover. You need to do it for you. You need to take this chance—you need to dance. And if you teach her to dance along the way too, it's your turn. You at least owe Jody that."

She thought about all of the smart-ass remarks she of rejoinder—none of them fit. This was one of those moments where she was out of her skin. This was his domain—this was heart to heart with nothing in between. Nothing to get in the way—it was sharpest razor's edge.

Her throat tightened. She just nodded and he let go. She knew he had won—she knew he was right this time. She could feel it.

07

AMANDA STOPPED IN the hallway at the line of vending machines. She looked at the apple, but thought the package of Pop Tarts would be a great thing to split with Samson as a peace offering for accidently kicking the server they shared to game when they were in brain freeze. The power cord had been marginal in reach and had tweaked when she kicked it. He had been playing in silent mode, was at level fifty-nine and about to kill the overlord, and then make it secure to level sixty and lock in a save game.

She opened her wallet to get a dollar out and a card fell out. She picked it up. It was the card that Jeff had given her two weeks before. "Crap." She had forgotten to call.

She bought two packs of Pop Tarts and the apple. Holding the card out, she returned to her cubicle. She reached around the gray carpeted wall and flipped the one pack of Pop Tarts onto his desk.

"I'm not going to share, toad."

She held the apple at the edge of the cubical wall. "I figured."

"I want half the apple… because I know you bought another packet of Tarts."

Amanda chuckled silently as her left hand slipped down and drew the knife on that side. A flick of her wrist and the apple was halved. She licked the knife and returned it to the scabbard in her boot. Her right hand grabbed the knife in her right boot—it was thinner and narrower, more of a stiletto—and stabbed the one-half and offered it at the wall edge.

The half disappeared. "Thanks. This way I can tell Tosika that you fed me healthy food."

"She won't believe you." She was distracted and chewed slowly as she studied the card. She had actually been in that office tower once. It was one of the taller more recently built high-rises downtown. She remembered dissing high-rise residents when she was trying to get away from this woman. If she were anything like Amanda—she would remember it for a long time.

She could hear Samson wheel back around the cubical wall. "Are you alright?"

Amanda just waved her hand with the apple part in it. "Yeah… just thinking."

"Well, don't do it so hard—it's starting to give me a headache."

Amanda put the apple down, put her headset on, and dialed the phone.

"Victoria Dumas's office."

It sounded so… official and daunting. Amanda hung up.

She sat looking at the phone as if it were a viper.

"You need to reach out as a friend, but you need it for you, too."

Amanda jumped. "What did you say?"

Samson wheeled around and looked at her scared face. "I didn't say a word." He studied her face. "Something's bothering you… and if you aren't going to talk to me, you need some time off to go talk to whoever it is you need to talk to."

Amanda thought for a moment and then turned back toward her desk. "Nah, I'm fine. Just trying to work out something. It's complicated."

The large man watched her fiddle with her mop of hair. He rolled back to his desk.

Amanda hit the re-dial button.

"Victoria Dumas's office."

It was the same voice. "Hello, this is Amanda Ruddy calling for Vic… um, Ms. Dumas."

"Yes, Amanda. I know she was expecting your call for the last few weeks. Unfortunately, she had an important meeting in Chicago. I expect her back on Monday. Would you care to leave a number where you can be reached or a cell number?"

Amanda panicked. Victoria knew where she drank… Amanda didn't want her to know where she worked, too. "No, no. That's okay. I'll call back next week." She hung up. *Fuck.*

Amanda looked at her computer screen. She clicked on the icon and entered the information for next Tuesday and hit save.

Tuesday was a lifetime away in Amanda's schedule.

The next time she looked up from the computer and print out schematics, Samson was gently moving her helmet from its shelf to her desk. He was only one of three people Amanda ever let touch her helmet.

"Traffic has cleared, it's now eight o'clock, and Tosika

will be home now. She got some nice ahi, yellowtail, and four sides of salmon skins, and she said hurry because the shrimp are crawling out of the sink."

Amanda looked up with an evil smirk. "You're inviting me over for sashimi?" The last time had been a disaster—she had some bad food at lunch, but it didn't manifest until Tosika had placed the raw fish on the low table.

"It wasn't your fault. Besides, today you only ate Pop Tarts and half an apple."

Suddenly, she was starving.

The two walked out with their helmets tucked under their right arms. The knives on his boots were custom-made by Samson's brother in Hawaii. A local artisan who specialized in Damascus steel and samurai folded steel blades had made hers. His expertise was making boot knives as well as the boots they fit into. She had the scabbard boots and knives made as a gift to herself for her one-year anniversary of sitting next to Samson.

After dinner, the quiet was thick and breathable. Amanda sat unusually frozen.

The small bag, strainer, and other tools for making real tea sat in front of Amanda. "This is close enough to your birthday and five years working with Samson. I know you like my tea but drink no tea at home. Now you can, Amanda-san." Tosika's voice tinkled and soothed at the same time. Amanda could listen to her talk all night long—but she rarely spoke more than a few words on any given night. A traditional family who, only begrudgingly, accepted her marriage to Samson had raised Tosika.

Amanda didn't know where to go with her emotions. She was touched by the gift, but more importantly, she was touched by the insight Tosika had shown and acted upon.

Amanda put her hands together and bowed deep and long. "*Domo arigato.*"

Samson lay back on the pillows. His face was a beaming smile, but his voice was a rumbling growl. "Don't you dare cry on that kimono you're wearing—it's hell getting stains out of that white cotton."

Amanda looked down at her tank top. She had never thought about what she wore. Her nipples were poking out shamelessly. She looked at Tosika's kimono and its formal white, sewn with delicate flowers. Suddenly, she was embarrassed by what she was wearing... but more importantly, she knew her nipples just got harder as she had a fleeting moment's thought about some other silk and how she wanted to touch it right then.

"You no listen to big kuma-san. You cry if you want or need to. I cry with you if it helps."

"No. I'm just..." She waved her hand about as she blushed. She didn't know what she was or how to say it. Her mind had just gone to a very complicated space that she wasn't equipped to process. It was a place where she had almost no experience—wanting another person.

"Hey, little one, it is okay. We understand. All we want is for you to be happy and enjoy a little. Just chill."

Amanda stood. Flustered, she retrieved her jacket. "I've got to run. I mean, it's late and, well..."

Samson and Tosika stood. "Relax, we understand. It was a long week. Just leave the stuff here and you can pick it up when you have your pack."

Amanda turned toward her bike and stopped. Her shoulders hunched and then fell. She turned back around. "Look, I appreciate all of this. I'm just kind of processing something right now..." She looked up at the two. "You two have been the greatest. And, Tosika, I was going to ask you about the tea. The rest of this is so great. Thank you." She hit a wall. She didn't know how to take where her mind was going. She started to turn. "Look, um, I'm just going to go now."

Tosika bowed slightly. "Goodnight, Amanda-san. Happy birthday."

Amanda bowed her head in a nod and walked to the bike. As she backed up, she remembered whose door it was. She pushed the kickstand down.

"I've got it." Samson was already moving the chain.

She looked at him with a begging. He closed his eyes and nodded his head once.

She backed into the night, started the bike and was gone. The light from the door got smaller until it was snipped out.

08

THE FLAMES DANCED on the steel. As the heat colored the sheet, the tiny banging made the flame dance. The flame snicked out, and Amanda held a steel block to the back as she bounced a small round-faced hammer on the face. Slowly, the lip was curling up and becoming more of a thin ridge. The hands danced back and forth from the flame to the hammering that formed the steel.

As the ridgeline grew into shape, Amanda could taste the real lips. They could feel how that fine line of the ridge was almost sharp but soft. Amanda looked at the mouth in steel and it wasn't the same—there had been the hint of the tip of her tongue. It had danced for a moment—but a moment that was carved in the yielding memories. Only the fourth woman Amanda had ever kissed. The memory drove her hands. The heat shaped the metal.

She walked around the large shape. The face was only three quarters there. The one side crawled back to almost hint at an ear. The hairline notched forward along the long side from the part and then rippled along the notch like separate strands of hair. Once she had massed the piece, she tipped it back flat on a pair of barrels and started adding mass to the trailing edges and letting them build into drops, and then just before the drops let go, she removed the heat and waved a hairdryer on the metal to stop the melt and turn it back to hard steel. When everything was perfect, she would braze bronze sheets the size of thumbprints onto the whole. It would take on the look of a painting done with a pallet knife but in bronze. The back or inside she would layer with thin copper sheeting and braze it down until it bonded. Then she would work the color from the heat until the dark blues and purples emerged. It was a physical representation of the darker inner self—and the lighter layers of the masks that we all wear for the public.

From any angle, the lips held her attention. She had meant for the empty eye sockets to be the focus—the windows to the soul. As she slowly stepped, the light glanced across the edge of the lip. She caught her breath… held it… and her body shook. She dropped into the chair. She had never experienced anything like it without touching herself. She sat in the sling chair, not moving, thinking of nothing— and everything.

Finally, she stared at the clock. It was still early. She knew what she needed to do. She washed the gloves off her hands and arms, pulled the old-school Bakelite goggles off her head, and peeled away layers of rough-out welding leather as she walked toward the shower.

Fifteen minutes later, she pulled the helmet on and clicked the chinstrap closed. Taking one more look at the statue, she hit the starter and slowly rolled out through the door.

09

THE MAN LIGHTLY rested his hand on Victoria's. They relaxed with the seats notched back. If there had been time to make reservations, a standard airline and first class would have been fine. But the last minute notice had precluded that, and they chartered a small Lear corporate jet. They would land and be in a car before the next available commercial plane would have even taken off.

Victoria was agitated and worried, but Paul's hand on hers always had a calming weight. A part of her mind thought back to law school. She had been accosted one night on her way back to the dorms from the library. At the student health clinic, a tall, dark-haired student volunteer sat studying at the reception. He had been reading a textbook as he waited out the Friday night. As she walked in with her clothes disheveled, he pushed his glasses up from the end of his nose and silently stood.

He never asked. He did not need to. He also knew the last person she wanted to talk to was a man. He stepped out of the front office and stood in the hall. "This way." He spoke in what he hoped was a composed, calming voice. He walked down the hall where Victoria was used to being seen for the usual student illnesses and boo-boos. He waved his hand to follow him. Finally, he led her into a small office with an examining table instead of a desk. "This will be more comfortable. Let me go get the nurse."

Victoria had grabbed his arm hard enough to leave marks. She was afraid. He never flinched. She had thought about how strange that was—that she had reached out to Paul—a man. She could never make heads or tails of why. But maybe somehow, she knew he truly cared for her well-being—even after only a few seconds.

He sat her down in the easy chair, and with his toe, he pulled the straight chair over. She continued to cling to his wrist and forearm. He sat quietly. "It's okay. You're safe here. I'll only step outside the door and then be right back in. Is that okay? Can I get the nurse for you?"

She held on for a minute more and then softened her grip. She nodded. True to his word, he was in plain sight the entire time.

She heard him talk to the male doctor. The doctor peeked in and then nodded. He left to get the nurse.

When Paul came back, he lifted her hand and put it back where it had been on his arm. Her whole world had been torn apart and nothing made sense—except holding onto him. He was calm and that provided her with something that felt akin to security.

Victoria had asked to have him beside her while the female nurse examined her and took samples. The nurse had convinced her it might be better to not.

A few days later, she couldn't stand hiding in her small apartment anymore, and she removed herself to the library.

She startled when the chair next to her moved. The student now wore thick black Clark Kent glasses. Without a word, he sat and softly placed his hand on hers. She'd calmed immediately.

"I don't even know your name…"

"Paul, Paul Peterson. I was happy to see you here. The weather's better here or outside than hiding in a closet, but any of the three can still be safe. They were safe a week ago, a month ago, and that first day you went away to college. That is the most important thing to hold in your mind."

"But—"

"No buts." He looked deep into her eyes. "Wherever your life takes you, you need to remember bad things are miniscule events. Every day you get up, have a nice day, and go to bed happy. Those days turn into weeks and months. Then you get a flat tire. If you let it, the flat tire destroys those months of good times. I'm not equating yesterday to a flat tire, but don't let it ruin or run your life moving forward. Don't let it define who you are. There are already too many victims in the world. Be the person you can be, have the potential to be, be proud of what your tombstone will say a long time from now—and live to that potential."

Victoria blinked. Softly, she nodded, "I don't even know your name… but you're here…"

"Yeah, I'm here. If you don't want me to be here, I'll go. But if you want me to be here, as a friend, I'll be here."

The friendship had taken time. At first, it was hard to process talking with a man. But with time, the scar of that night dimmed, and the light of their friendship brightened. Massive study marathons took up an entire cafeteria table with one on each end, food wrappers mixed in the middle with used coffee cups. Cracking books slowly became walks and talks to and from classes, which eventually became walks along the shoreline and talks about life away from their studies.

Over the years, they had talked their way through the part about being friends but not lovers. He had never looked to be the latter. He had only felt the draw to be the former. She never saw or heard about him having a girlfriend or even dating. Eventually, he admitted the thought had never occurred to him.

They became a constant pair through law school. The third year, they shared a flat and covered the walls with study notes. They had both been drawn to international business law, and after they sat at the bar side by side, they sat down for fun and drew up the four-pound tome that was their partnership agreement, along with two other students who they knew were roped in as associates for only two years. Since that time, the list of names on their door had grown to almost the floor. They had been the preferred council for the new owners of the office tower. The holding company was impressed with their work and had retained them—with the three floors being part of the deal. They didn't want the firm relocating.

Victoria stirred and reached forward for her soda water. She glanced at Paul. She knew that look. "What fond memory are you running through that fuzzy head of yours?"

He smiled but didn't open his eyes. "Remembering that Christmas we drove you home to visit your folks."

Victoria groaned and leaned back into her chair. "Oh, what a wonderful disaster that was."

"Whose side of the family was that cousin from?"

Victoria snorted. "The Neanderthal side."

"Oh, come now. He had at least another two inches before the knuckles touched the carpet. But the drooling was a bit excessive." They both smiled. "Do you think your mother was serious about the possibility of a match there?"

"I'm afraid that Mother Dear still says five Hail Marys, ten Our Fathers, and goes through at least a couple of rites of attrition every morning since the day she saw me kiss Becky Roland on the lips." Then she remembered why they were going to Nashell. She leaned back and thought about her mother. They had not been as close as they could have been, but she was going to miss what little they had these last few years. "Well... I'm sure she used to."

The plane cruised through the clouds on its way to Naples, Florida. The weather was clear and calm. Comfortable and relaxed, the two passengers dozed.

Paul stirred. "Did you talk to that woman or at least, leave her a message?"

"She never left her phone number."

"So all you have is the bar in the Pearl?"

"Karen said she called and told her she was expecting me back tomorrow."

Paul groaned. "Well, we could send a couple of interns down to try to find the bar again... but I'm not confident we would ever get them back."

Victoria pinched the bridge of her nose. "No, no... I will take care of it when we get back. Right now, it's a distraction that I don't need."

10

AMANDA SLAPPED THE ticket down on the desk. It wasn't her first ticket, but it was the first she had gotten by being predictable. The rage boiled away inside. She carefully placed her helmet on its secure shelf—away from anywhere she may throw something. She grabbed her safety scissors and put them to her hair that was poking in and out of the lower part of her ear. She thought a moment and then looked around the cubical wall. The oversized chair was empty.

Storming down the cubical alley, she looked for someone who didn't have their head down—hiding from the wrath of the storming Amanda. Some had seen her at work. Some had been recipients of her razor-sharp tongue. The reasons she still had her job was Samson, and the fact that she had never done anything physically to anyone that was harmful. The nerf catapult and the nerf crossbow were the extent of her reaching out with any violence—and the standard of nerd warfare once squirt guns were outlawed.

She crouched and jumped straight up, landing with both

boots on an empty cubical desk. On the other side of the back cubical wall, a frightened young girl looked up in alarm at the loud noise. She beheld an angry visage of an avenging Valkyrie in a white ribbed tank top, pointing a threatening finger at her.

"You!" Amanda oozed out in her best snake woman Halloween voice. "What's your name?"

"K… Kate," the newbie squeaked.

"Move and ten-thousand trolls and their war slime will invade your cubical and trample any code you write in the next ten million years." The Valkyrie disappeared only to be replaced with the sound of a desk chair racing down the alleyway. As the chair neared Kate, Amanda leaped over the seat and fell into it as it came to a stop.

Kate wasn't sure if the Cheshire cat smile was playful or about to eat her.

"Female." Amanda looked her over. "How long have you worked here?"

Kate's eyes returned to normal, but not her voice. She still squeaked. "About a month… long enough…" she gulped, "…to know who you are."

Amanda waved off either the compliment or insult— she didn't care which. "Don't believe everything you hear— it's probably either all true or only half as bad as the truth."

Amanda held up the scissors—Mickey Mouse ear handles out. "I need you to cut some hair." With her left hand, she grabbed the stray bit that was offending her. "This shit is getting in my ear."

Kate started to cut and then leaned back. "Why don't you go to a salon?"

Amanda growled. "Cut."

Three snips and the offenders were removed. Kate returned the scissors.

Amanda stood and glared at the three sets of eyes that were jammed into the tight corners of eyes now looking at the crazy woman. She growled at the nerds. "Eat code or die." All eyes quickly focused on monitors.

She turned toward the young woman and softened. Her voice dropped to just between the two of them. "Look, thanks… and welcome to hell and heaven on earth. If any of these swinging dicks give you any…" She swung her head around the cluster as she growled. "And I do mean *any* grief—you come see Samson or me. *Capiche?*"

The girl nodded.

"Good girl." Amanda spun on her heel and strolled off.

Kate's eyes wandered down the leathered legs and stopped at the sight of the two large knives scabbarded in the tall boots. Her eyes went back to the bunny in headlights mode.

The hair was out of Amanda's ear—now to deal with the rest of the day.

As she strolled back up her cubical alley with a steaming mug of coffee, she saw Samson sitting in the middle of the alley holding the long yellow piece of paper. *Fuck.* Her attitude was balanced on the brink.

"Do I need to start picking you up in the morning? Or just have Tosika call you earlier?" The man sat, deadpan, but Amanda could see the twinkling in his eyes. They both knew there was no time clock anywhere in the building—or the overtime would match the national debt by the second quarter. With most of the workers, it was a matter of maintaining a routine, or with some, it was just a simple case of obsessive compulsive diarrhea—the shit that you do routinely in your life—like always being at work at 8:14 in the morning.

Amanda snatched the ticket from his fingers as his big brother laugh started. "Scooter cop. He said he used to be in a patrol car but just transferred. He was waiting for me on the west end of the park. I guess I'd lost him a few times before, and he figured out that quarter mile of running path I used as a shortcut."

Samson was shaking but still tried to be the older brother. "I *told* you one day you'd either take out a slow runner or get caught. Was the guy laughing?"

"Yeah… he was pretty cool… but he still wrote me the ticket." She sat down and duck lipped as she looked at the ticket. "He actually asked me not to cut through there anymore."

"Asked you?"

"Even said *please*… well, okay… he said it would probably please the walkers and runners if I didn't race through their pathway."

"I'll bet they would."

"I've never seen anyone in there before."

Samson laughed as he turned back toward his desk. "They probably heard you coming."

"Don't talk nasty, sensei. Nobody hears Ninja Girl coming."

The big man smiled as they both went back to work. The two keyboards became echoes of the others around them. The only sound was the occasional ball in a thoughtful mitt or the squish of a squeezy toy.

"Sandwich run—anyone need, want, or adore anything from the one-armed bandits?"

The sound of the midafternoon cry for food, or *just shoot me now*, caused Amanda to shrink the five windows she had been working in on the three monitors, leaving the second screen empty except for the yellow pulsing alert.

She stared at the note. Her mind was still buried somewhere in a lower level of the chip that had been consuming her life for the past year. The words had no meaning.

The soft sound of the chair skateboarding behind her registered as Samson returned from overseeing something down the alley. He spun and rebounded back to directly behind her.

"Are you going to call her? Because I'm getting kind of starved, and if I have to wait much longer for lunch, I may just pull one of your knives and go to lunch on your right leg."

Amanda slowly spun and looked at the man. "You really want to try that? Really? Use your own fucking knives, troll."

"Are you really going to call her? Really?"

The memory slid sideways and Amanda's eyes popped open.

Samson chuckled silently. "Yeah... *that* phone call."

Amanda glanced at her wristwatch... 3:42. "Fuck."

"Too late?"

She spun around. "I don't know." She hung the headset on her ears and adjusted the microphone as she called up her personal address book and hit the green dial icon.

"Thank you for calling Abbot, Brunk, Dumas and Peterson. How may I direct your call?"

"Victoria Dumas, please."

"One moment."

"Victoria Dumas's office, this is Karen."

Amanda hung her head into her upturned hand. "Hi, this is Amanda Ruddy calling for Ms. Dumas..."

"Yes, Amanda. Victoria was looking forward to your call. I did expect her back today, but she and Paul delayed in returning and took some personal time. If you can give me your phone nu…"

Amanda stared at the red phone icon of the hung up call. Her finger still hovered over the left mouse key.

Five words seared through her mind. *She and Paul*, and *personal time*. It was everything she needed to know. Everything else with this woman had been a tease. If she was taking time with her girlfriend or getting married to her life partner… but her taking personal time with some guy…

She started to stand and reach for her helmet. The massive hand on her right forearm pulled her back down into the chair. She ripped the headset off and threw it at the center monitor as she spun around. Her eyes were burning. Her nose seared and stung. She could not take a breath.

The man was all about calm. His hand still rested on her arm as his chair slid forward—his massive legs trapping hers between. He all but smothered her in a bear hug. His voice was a soft rumble from deep beneath his heart. "Whatever happened just now… the last place you need to be is on a motorcycle. You need to settle down and just breathe."

Amanda's body started to vibrate. Fear and anger warred for the nerves.

"Slow, deep breaths—breathing is our friend."

She was off vacationing with a dude. She was off vacationing with a dude.

She was off vacationing with a dude.

"Amanda… Amanda." Samson was snapping his fingers in her face. She reached up and grabbed.

"What…?" Her voice sounded distant even to her.

He studied her, waiting.

"What?"

"You've been out of it for twenty minutes. You've just been sitting there mumbling something about a dude."

"She's off somewhere with a dude."

"Yeah, something like that."

"No. Victoria. She ran off somewhere with a boyfriend."

He thought about the implications. "Are you sure it was a dude? I mean some names are kind of iffy in the gender."

"Paul. The dudes name is Paul. Not even a diesel dyke would go by Paul."

"Good point." He reached into his back pocket and fished out his cell phone. The giant thumb hit the screen with one swipe and then held down to make it dial the one number that was his end-all-be-all.

He watched Amanda as he listened to the voice. In Japanese, he told the person on the other end, "The dungeon is closed tonight. I'm bringing Amanda home for the night." He hung up.

Amanda knew very little, but she got the drift of the statement. "You don't have to—"

"You have no say in the matter. Just call the Trolls and I will call the Wizards and we'll leave early. We need to go to the market and pick up a few things if I'm cooking fish tacos tonight."

11

"SHE JUST HUNG up on me."

"What did you tell her, Karen?"

"Exactly what you told me to tell her, Ms. Dumas. I told her that you—oh…"

Victoria pinched the bridge of her nose as she listened to her secretary realize what her wording had exactly been. "Exactly what did you tell her?"

"I told her that you were looking forward to her call, but that you and Mr. Peterson… but that isn't what I said—"

"What did—"

"I used his first name."

Victoria frowned as she looked at Paul. "But Paul always insists that people use his first name. He's been doing that for as long as I've known… him." She suddenly realized what her secretary had already realized.

The older woman's voice sounded soft and distant. "She thinks this is a romantic tryst."

"Oh… fuck." Victoria's face buried fully in her hand.

"What did you say?" The woman on the phone was the

echo of the man in the room.

"You both heard what I said." Victoria blushed. "It just seemed like the right word for the moment. Moreover, I will swear to that under oath. Oh, God, I can't believe… this can't get any worse."

"When is the funeral?"

"We're having a small viewing tonight and then just a graveside in the morning. Mom outlived most of her friends, or they moved away to the big cities, and I have no idea how to get in touch with them. We searched the house this morning, but there was no personal address book or anything that we could find."

"Wouldn't she have all of that on her phone or on her computer?"

"The easiest way to explain my mother, Karen, would be to tell you that her only phone is in the kitchen. It is black, weighs about twenty pounds, and sits hulking on the counter next to the white and yellow pages—"

The older woman laughed. "Oh no… and it's a rotary dial, right?"

"You got it in one."

"When are you planning to come back?"

"I'm not sure what condition her estate was in. I don't even know if she had a will or what. It'll probably be at least a week, maybe two."

"Is Mr. Peterson staying?"

"He says he won't leave me in a lurch, so if you could tell Lynnette, then they can coordinate what he has on his docket, too."

"Of course… She's my next meeting. But what can I do to help with Amanda?"

"I'm not sure. I don't even know what the bar was

called. It's just an old dive bar on the edge of the Pearl and almost into the Northwest industrial area. It took me an hour to find it again the first time."

"Okay, we'll just have to play it as it unfolds."

"Oh, I'm pretty sure she's never calling again. I know I wouldn't."

"I'm so sorry."

"It's not your fault. This all goes back to my running when I should have stood my ground or at least gotten a phone number."

"Okay, but I still feel like I let you down."

"You're fine. You are the best personal assistant I could ever ask for. One way or another, it'll work out."

"But she sounded nice."

"She is. But it's now up to me."

"Well, keep me posted."

"Will do. We'll talk tomorrow."

"Goodnight, y'all." Her secretary laughed.

Victoria chuckled as she hung up and turned off her phone. *Why did everyone think that if your parents live in the South, you talk Southern?*

"So she thinks we are off on a romantic escape to exotic Florida." Victoria closed her eyes tiredly. Her body ached from mental exhaustion. She softly nodded and then looked over at her longtime friend.

He smiled wanly. "Bad assumption."

"You know... I've run so hard in my life, I've rarely had this opportunity to slow down and realize how special certain people truly are."

Paul adjusted in the large flower-print chair. "How do you mean?"

Victoria looked at how comfortable Paul was in the

chair. It was rare when he could sit in a chair that fit him. This one just needed to be reupholstered in leather to match his office, and shipped back to Portland. It would make a great Christmas gift for him. She smiled softly.

"Vic…?"

She shook and looked up. "Sorry, I was just thinking of something else. No, I have always valued Karen as an exceptional administrative assistant. Her professionalism has been truly amazing. Through her divorce these last three years, no matter how ugly it got, no matter how she felt, she'd hit the front door with a smile and there was nothing but upbeat, good professional cheer. She's buoyed me as well as my clients through the thick and thin of things.

"But with that conversation, I realized—she's never questioned my motives or my personal feelings. Heck, even I don't know where I stand sexually—other than knowing I didn't like being raped." They both smiled wanly. "I don't know if Amanda is what I'm looking for or even if I'm—"

"A lesbian?"

She caved with a sigh. "Yes… I have no basis. But I have… I mean, I find her… Oh, heck—I liked her kissing me." She looked up. "I liked it a lot. I felt… safe—and liked."

His voice was soft as a whisper. "Loved?"

She sat for a moment and then nodded. *Loved.*

12

THE PROFESSIONAL-LOOKING WOMAN with the gray seasoning in her hair picked her way daintily through the tables as she made her way to the bar. The bartender calmly polished the beer glass as he watched her move. She might have been in a bar before, but if she had, it was many long years since then.

Jeff made his living reading people. Mostly it was about whether they were too drunk to drive home, but also, it was about why the person was in his bar or who they were. This woman was a matched set for the younger woman who came looking for Amanda. Except this woman could be Amanda's mother. He guessed they worked together at the law office. This one's clothes were professional, but not expensive. He guessed personal assistant.

She reached the bar and started to speak.

"No." He stopped her with his hand—palm out.

He leaned over and placed the glass in the freezer. Standing, he spun the towel and then snapped it over his shoulder. He pointed toward a table at the sunnier end of the bar. "Go sit." She frowned and he nodded his head as if she was an errant child. "Go."

He reached into the cooler for a glass and beer and then thought. Turning, he grabbed two mugs and the coffee pot.

The tray had a container of sweeteners and a tiny pitcher of cream alongside the two mugs of coffee. Jeff placed it gently on the table and moved one mug in front of the quiet woman. Setting the rest out on the table, he laid the tray on the next table, turned a chair around and sat backward, straddling the chair with his arms crossed on the table.

He watched the woman. Her face was as businesslike as his. Nothing was going to be given freely. Everything would be *quid pro quo*—you share, I'll share.

Jeff gently picked up a packet of sweetener and mixed it into his coffee with a shot of the milk. Taking a sip as he watched her add half a pack of pink and a touch of milk, Jeff watched over the rim of his mug. "Amanda."

"Amanda." She nodded. "And Victoria… my boss."

Jeff put down his mug and ran his hand over his bristly chin as he thought. "Where is she?"

"She's out of state on some personal business."

"With some dude…"

"Her best friend since school, and her business partner—not a lover. In the seven years I have worked for Ms. Dumas, I have never heard of either even having a lunch date, much less a relationship."

Jeff thought that over as the woman took a few sips of coffee. The late sun clawed its way down the tree-lined street. The soft light that bounced off the buildings across the street played compassionately on her face. Jeff could see the pain of her own and some hard years that belied her age. The woman knew about heartless years and the hope that came from a possible friendship—that could be more.

"That's a lot of information—personal information—for a secretary to be sharing about her boss."

"Personal assistant—the secretaries are in the pool. My job is to look after my boss. Through a slip of my tongue, I failed that job. I'm here to lay the groundwork for the next move to be more than successful."

Jeff nodded. "How did you find me?"

She smiled. "There are nine bars that met the qualifications. You were number seven."

"How much beer did you have to drink?"

"One beer and two of something called PPR."

"It's PBR. It stands for… never mind—it's not important. So what did you have in mind?"

She smiled and took another sip of her coffee. She knew she had him recruited, and she might even have a nice new friend and a quiet place to come talk.

"I take it you're the owner here…" She looked around at all of the early twentieth-century wood fixtures in the bar, and smiled, relaxed, warm. "This reminds me of my father somehow. Is it always this quiet?"

"Your father was a barkeep?"

She shook her head as she sipped the coffee. "No, he worked in the floating dry dock. He was a welder. He put in long, hard hours from dawn until three. He'd stop off for a beer with his friends and then arrive home about five to help me with homework before dinner. I think in all the years that he stopped off, he only finished a drink once. It was the day they shot JFK. They closed the dock at eleven when they heard. The bar was full, and they were listening to the radio."

Jeff nodded. "I think there was a lot of drinking that

day." *Shared memories.*

Karen looked out the large, but somehow dim, windows at a time many decades before—the silent hum of the bar's voices long past, helped that memory. The coffee was warm and felt good in her mouth. The mug wasn't one of those prissy ones that people thought a woman with gray hair should be drinking from—this was the kind her father drank from—thick, heavy, aged white, and substantial. *An honest vessel of servitude—like her father.* The chipped white mug was an icon of her growing up and reading to her father while sitting on his lap as he leisurely drank his evening coffee after dinner. It felt… right. She sipped again.

She cleared the history from her throat and turned toward the barkeep. "What's the best time on Sundays?"

He studied her. He had a feeling they were long past the conversation of Amanda and this woman's boss. He took a sip of his coffee. Carefully putting the mug down on the table, he touched the tip of his tongue along his lips and then rolled them together. "I open the bar at eleven. I have a small rush right after church, but by two-thirty the place is empty until about four. The chili is at its peak about three, and if you call around one, I make a mean biscuit from my grandmother's secret recipe. Her mother was a child baker during the California gold rush and made more gold than most of the miners."

Karen smiled. "I think I'm going to start enjoying my weekends again."

"Good company would be nice for a change."

Karen nodded and put her mug down with a contented smile. "Now about our girls…"

13

THE LARGE BUZZER at the door jarred Amanda's hand. The torch waved away from the bronze as it flowed out in a small puddle. She reached over and grabbed the lead hammer and smacked the solidifying puddle of molten metal. The pool flattened and grew a frayed edging. Some would become grounded or sanded off, but the rest would resemble crude stucco.

She pushed the goggles up on her head as she turned off the torch. Striding toward the door, she glanced at the clock. She unsnapped the leather jacket and pulled it off in one movement. The jacket hit the only window in the building's office area, next to the door. Her tits stood out just below the top of the welding apron. There had been no need for a T-shirt, pants, or panties. She grabbed up her tall stainless steel coffee mug and guzzled the tepid coffee on her way to the door. Banging the mug down on the small desk, she stepped to the door in her boots and leather apron and pondered whether she should open it. She wasn't sure she wanted to deal with Sam this morning. She glanced at the big office clock—she realized clocks were everywhere in her life, and yet, she did not have to keep to a strict timetable.

As she reached for the doorknob, she could hear Sam outside. "If you so much as reach for those fucking knives, you will need a new place to live."

She jerked the door open and turned to walk back to where her coffee was. "What the fuck do you want? I'm busy, and now I have to go to work."

"I'd pay good money to see you ride off dressed just like that."

She knew he was looking at her butt. Everything about her was hard muscle and tight—except her small rounded butt that jiggled ever so slightly—no matter how much she tried to tighten the cheeks up. She was still self-conscious about that one thing.

She slurped the last of the coffee as she clenched and unclenched her cheeks. The show was amusing for her and the man she knew was only interested in butt—not necessarily hers, or even a woman's—he just liked butts almost as much as he liked large tits.

"Twat Twin called. The wedding is in two weeks and you haven't responded."

Amanda turned, malevolently holding her stainless steel mug just below her mouth. "I couldn't find a dress."

"So don't wear one."

"Go naked. Yeah, Twat Twin would love that."

"Fuck it. You wear the tux, I'll wear a dress, and we'll switch sides."

She thought about the offer that she knew was serious. Sam was not gay or even a drag queen. He was just amicable. Sam wanted peace in the only family he had left. His mother had died when he was eight and Amanda's family took him and his eleven-year-old sister in. The first two years, they slept on the funky foldout couch bed. Later, Amanda had started kicking one of their asses off the couch on occasion and made them sleep in her real bed, and she took the couch with the other. Other nights, her twin had done the same. It was either a clusterfuck or a merry-go-round in the small two-bedroom house, but they were all together. Amanda's parents were easygoing college professors who were smart enough to let the four kids work it out.

Amanda put the empty mug down and turned off the coffee maker. "Sorry, but it just isn't going to happen."

"I had to try."

She pulled the apron up over her head as she moved toward the shower area. "Ever the hopeful Sam." She tossed the apron and started hopping around as she pulled off her boots. "Gotta run, Sam."

He waved as he backed out—smiling. "Yeah, I gotta go..." then his voice turned to a mutter, "...take a cold shower." The vision of her compact tits jiggling as she jumped her hard body around was seared into his brain. *Hot butt and tits—it is going to be a grand Wednesday.*

Sam smiled as he quietly closed Amanda's door, strode the four steps to his office door and entered his sanctuary. The electronics array looked more like a spaceship. Where Amanda was a genius about the inner-workings of computers—Sam was a genius at making them do his bidding. Still pictures or video, Sam loved manipulating and creating. His first love was pornography because it has to do with the human form. But most of his money now came from finalizing images for highly successful photographers.

His other love was inventing. He held many patents for surveillance cameras and software. Everything he invented was field trialed on his buildings—especially, all the cameras that monitored the street activities around the buildings.

As he sat, he glanced at the feeds from several cameras and noticed a woman on one of the sidewalks. The figure was standing in the mouth of Amanda's alley that led to her garage door. He snorted to himself as he thought about what the black leather motorcycle would look like as she raced out of the building to work.

He turned back to the image he was photoshopping on the thirty-inch monitor.

Out on the street, the slender wrist turned and exposed the smooth lines of the gold watch. *Perfect timing.*

Victoria looked up and nodded as she turned into the small alleyway. She noted there were no trash containers she normally equated with an alley. The narrow slot between buildings ended at a large metal roll-up door that was a combination of peeled black paint and galvanized steel. As she walked, the fact that the entire length looked swept and washed did not escape her—nor had the newer concrete of the sidewalk and gently sloped egress onto the street. None of these factors fit the industrial neighborhood. She was now very confident in the map and information that Karen had given her.

Now it was just down to the final bit of exacting detail about the time.

As she stopped a car-length from the door, she smiled. She heard the door start to rise as the motorcycle started.

Victoria stood her ground, her hands on her hips. Somehow, she felt like she was supposed to have a pair of six-shooters strapped to them. This was the showdown. It all stopped here.

Amanda pulled her helmet onto her head as the door

began to rise. Her left hand turned the key as her right thumb pressed the starter and twisted the throttle. Her left heel pushed back the kickstand and braced as the right toe snicked the transmission into first gear.

The door was four feet up and there were shoes in the alleyway. As the door rose, Amanda watched the legs, and then the skirt appear. The stance was pure gunslinger. Her hands rested on the hips, relaxed but ready. The white of the silk blouse shone in the morning light. Deep crescent shadows accentuated the large breasts. The soft flow of loose blonde curls flowed around her face and just kissed the top of her breasts loosely above the nipples that showed firm in anticipation.

Amanda's eyes locked onto Victoria's upper lip. Her mind took her on a ride along the ridge. The reflected morning sunshine glowed softly at the ridge of the upper border, red.

Amanda's heart stopped and then stuttered.

She eased the clutch and the bike rolled forward. As she cleared the door, the radio frequency identifier triggered the switch and the door began to roll down. Amanda's toe snicked the transmission into neutral and she glided to a stop.

The two women faced off, neither moving.

"What are you doing here?"

The words were muffled by the full face helmet. Victoria held her hand up to her ear.

Amanda pulled the helmet off as Victoria walked to the side of the motorcycle.

Amanda growled. "What the fuck are you doing here?"

Victoria reached up and softly cupped the sides of Amanda's head. She reached into the hair and around the ears. Her green eyes burned into the brown of the other. She leaned close. Her breath was warm on Amanda's face. "I came to make my intentions known in a way that you would not misconstrue."

She leaned in, and as their lips touched, the thin line melded with the other. Their lips parted as the slender tip of her tongue tasted Amanda.

Amanda's right arm reached out and around the silk at her waist. Victoria leaned in against the leather pant-leg and her legs parted until she had gripped the other's thigh.

The lips retreated only partially as the tongues gently invaded the other. It was a bashful battle mixed in the torrid air of their panting breaths.

"But you were off with some dude."

"A friend," Victoria panted. "Not a lover." She leaned deeper into the kiss. Urging her body to blend with the woman on the motorcycle—she was aware of the feeling that she had never experienced as she rubbed against the leg in the leather pants. She did not know if it was the leather, the leg, or if it was just because it was attached to the woman she could not get out of her mind. She only knew she didn't want any of the feelings to stop.

Amanda shied back. "I have to—"

Victoria put her index finger on Amanda's mouth. "If you call in sick, I'll call in sick… and that's my boss, Paul, standing at the end of the alley."

Amanda leaned so she could see around Victoria's curls. The tall man in the dark suit stood bashfully with his hands in his pockets. His right hand came out and waved once as he smiled.

"He's the—"

"The dude I was with, yes. Best friends since college…

but never anything else." She nodded.

"I tried the *take it slow* approach and we both know how that turned out. I've had a lot of time to think about this. I don't know where I am or what I'm doing. But there are a few things that I do know… and I think I'm sure about them.

"Look, there's a lot to tell you. You can hear it from me, or you can hear it from him—either way, it'll be the same. I would rather you hear it from me." She hesitated, and then plunged in with both feet. "In my bed or yours…"

Amanda's brown eyes studied the woman's green. Then she saw the tip of a tiny tongue as it slid across the ridge of the upper lip. She remembered what was in the middle of her loft.

"It better be your bed. The maid didn't show up this week, and the place is a mess."

Victoria leaned in for a longer kiss. As her breath shortened, she pulled away. "Stay close, I think I feel the three-day flu coming on."

Amanda smiled. "I thought it was something I ate last night, but maybe it's just something I haven't eaten—yet."

14

AMANDA NEVER THOUGHT about someone living and working in the same high-rise building—but then, it wasn't much different than her studio/home/garage. And if your office takes up three floors, the package deal on an extra apartment or something would probably be a sweet deal as well.

She pulled up at the valet stand behind Victoria and watched her get out. She spoke to the guy as he looked back at the all-black figure and motorcycle grumbling at the curb. Finally, he nodded and walked back toward Amanda.

"Follow me into the garage, and you will see a couple of motorcycles parked to your right. Park your motorcycle anywhere in the striped zone—as soon as I park Ms. Dumas's car, I'll be right back and show you where you can lock up your helmet."

Amanda nodded and followed him through the security door. She found the motorcycle area and was impressed. There were even bang bars poured into the concrete of the wall to lock the bike onto. She saw the large lockers but didn't see any way to open them. The valet ran back down around the ramp.

"Hi, I'm Manny. The flat-track hog is mine."

Amanda gave a low whistle. "I was just admiring the paint."

He looked at her nebula helmet. "What I was going for was what you have on your helmet. Now I see how far I fell short." He fished a small clutch of cards out of his pocket.

"The guy who did this was an astrophysicist first and a painter."

"The dude poured his soul into it. It looks like the crab nebula."

"You aren't even close by a million light years. The star cluster is the Owl Cluster in the Cassiopeia nebula."

Manny thought about it and then smiled. "The owl… just like the V-Max—unassuming, yet very deadly. I like the way this guy thinks."

Amanda nodded. "Look, I'd like to shoot the shit with you about bikes and nebulas, but…"

"Sorry, I could tell you and Ms. Dumas are running late." He waved one of the cards by the locker marked with a nine, and the door popped open about an inch. He turned and handed her the card. "Forty-five is divisible by the sum of its parts—nine. You get it close, even with it in your shirt pocket, it'll open. Don't lose the card—it takes me a week to make a new one."

Amanda stuck the card in her back pocket and carefully stowed the helmet in the locker. She closed the door and felt it draw closed magnetically. She turned. "Thanks."

"No problem. That's your locker for as long as you need it."

Amanda studied him.

"Ms. Dumas is a very special lady. I'd take a bullet for her. She gave me a chance when nobody else would and got me this job…" He stalled.

Amanda understood completely. He'd also protect her against any ill will. She thought about Samson. Amanda reached out and gripped the man's shoulder and looked him in the eyes. "I understand—truly, I do. All of it—I was there once." He nodded.

Victoria was waiting in the vestibule when they returned, examining a handful of mail. As Amanda walked up, she turned and led the way to the elevators. She was all business.

As they stepped into the elevator, the door closed. Victoria leaned in, gave Amanda a hard kiss, and then stepped back. "Don't say a word until we're in the apartment." They stood looking at the door like two drones.

Amanda eyed the slow changing numbers. At the twenty-first floor, the car stopped. The doors opened to a little lady who looked like she was dressed for church. In her arms, she held a tiny black poodle. She had a slightly surprised look on her face but entered hesitantly.

Victoria nodded to the lady as she pushed the button for the twenty-fifth floor. "Good morning, Mrs. Abbot."

The woman watched the shiny steel doors but nodded in Victoria's direction. "Victoria." Her eyes never left the reflection of the black leather figure topped by a mop of brown hair. As the doors started to slide open, she glanced down and saw the two knives sticking out of the sides of the boots. Her head whipped around as her eyes got very big. She glanced over to Victoria. "Oh, my…" The doors were sliding shut as Victoria smiled and nodded at the woman.

Amanda mumbled, "Fuck."

Victoria giggled softly. "No… fuck her… and her prig of a son." Her head snapped around with a mock horror look on her face, and then dramatically looked down at the knife handle facing her. "Oh, my goodness… we have a terrorist in the building." She looked back up at Amanda with a smirk and wiggled her eyebrows before the business face snapped back on as the door opened again.

Amanda noticed the large 'P' illuminated. She almost didn't follow Victoria out of the elevator—she felt the urge to run while she could. She was in way over her head. She squeaked, "This is the penthouse."

Victoria turned, afraid she would be watching the doors closing on the other woman as she ran away. She stood looking into scared brown eyes. She also noticed the one boot was jammed into the side of the doorway—trapping the doors open. She stepped back and stood close.

Reaching her two hands gently to the sides of Amanda's face, she softly kissed her. "You have to trust me that it's okay if I am to trust you that I'm safe." The moment lasted for several long heartbeats. "After all… it's not like I have the whole floor. Each of the partners has an apartment here. It makes it convenient."

She spun and left the choice to Amanda. As she waved her passkey at the door, she turned. "I only have half the space." She pushed the door open as she smiled.

Amanda rolled her eyes, stepped out of the elevator and followed.

As the large door clicked quietly shut, Victoria turned around to Amanda and laced her fingers into the mop of hair as she pressed her mouth hungrily to Amanda's. Her body stiffened as her breasts molded around the firmer and smaller ones. Her tongue probed along the teeth and danced as both women were caught up in their first hard kiss. Neither breathed.

Finally, their mouths separated from the built-up nervousness. The leather squeaked as Victoria's open hand dragged across Amanda's strong back—searching for purchase and rubbing in the desperation of release. Amanda's arms circled low. Working against the silk, her one hand slid down to draw over the soft round butt that clinched firm at her touch. She drew in steady against the other crotch with only a hint of hesitant grinding. Victoria's body succumbed to the heat. Any thought was long gone as primal urges took over.

Amanda's hand crawled up the silk blouse and then flattened as it felt the sensation of the slippery surface. Finally reaching the soft clouds of curls, she grabbed and spun the other woman around and against the wall as she used her whole body to pin her there. Amanda's left leg cautiously slid between Victoria's exposed knees and lower thighs. The body beneath her became electric as her upper leg ground hard against the linen-covered crotch. Their breathing came in pants as the kisses became harder and longer, deeper.

Slowly, one leather hip moved forward and began to grind between the skirt-covered legs. Amanda heard the catch in Victoria's breath as her body stiffened and bowed out from the wall with her own pressure. Trapping the leather leg, the two had their own rhythm as a low whimper rose in the lawyer's throat. All sense or need of social propriety slipped away... *the privacy of one's home...*

Amanda moved breathless from Victoria's mouth and ran her tongue hungrily along her jaw. The scent of citrus filled her nose. She traced a wet line up to the small gold stud earrings and then began to nibble. Her ears proved sensitive, and as she squirmed, Amanda moved to tracing the outer rim of her ear that was playing hide-and-seek in the soft curls.

Victoria rolled her head away slightly, making her neck an easier target for the searching, teasing tongue. The blossoming heat released the soft scent of yesterday's perfume. Her skin felt electrified wherever Amanda's tongue landed. The very edges of her senses tingled as they never had before, and the blood roared in her ears. She wanted to be consumed with this woman's touch, tongue, mouth—whatever it took to be completely dominated by the sensations Amanda pulled out of her.

Amanda's tongue rode around the top of the ear as she whispered, "You're mine."

The reaction was anything but what she had expected.

Victoria's eyes flew open and she started to scream, but there was no air to make noise. Her panic became physical as her arms grabbed Amanda's hair and leather and pulled and pushed as she shuddered with violence. As Amanda stumbled back, she could see that Victoria was shaking in sheer terror. Her eyes were open but saw nothing. Her arms still flailed at the air. Her legs lost their fight with gravity and she sank to the floor, gasping for air as she began to cry.

Amanda had seen programmers go into panic attacks from losing days' worth of coding, but she had no idea what she could do for the woman she so desperately wanted to help now. Victoria wasn't flopping around like what she imagined being an epileptic attack. She was just—not there.

Suddenly, Amanda realized where she was. She jerked the door open and then realized if the door closed, she would be unable to get back in. Pulling the knife from her boot, she struck with all of her might in the wooden door. The knife buried almost a full inch into the hardwood. The door closed against the knife and Amanda turned to the elevator.

There were no buttons… only a sensor pad.

Amanda rushed back into the penthouse and searched Victoria's purse. *Nothing.*

She turned and looked at the skirt. There were no pockets.

She returned to the purse and pulled out the woman's wallet. Scanning through the credit cards—all of them were black or muted silver, all with gold printing and a logo—except one. Amanda pulled out the single matte black card.

She turned it over. It was blank. She held it up and looked at the edge. It was a sandwich of carbon black separated by a thin line of copper. *RFID* radio frequency identification—the same as the card Manny had given her for the helmet locker.

She shoved the card in her back pocket and kneeled in front of Victoria. "I don't know if you can hear me, but I'm going to go get help. I'll be right back. It's going to be all right."

She stood and raced for the elevator.

Once in the elevator, she stood looking at the triple row of buttons. She could not even start to guess which floor she needed. Then she remembered the old lady. She poked the twenty-fifth-floor button and the twenty-first. The gentle lowering was maddeningly slow as the elevator dropped the ten floors.

The doors opened and Amanda held the door as she stepped out. There was nothing but apartment doors in both directions. She stepped back in. The doors crawled closed and the downward motion resumed.

The doors opened to a repeat of the floor above. Amanda didn't understand. She stepped back and took a long deep breath… and pushed *lobby*.

As the elevator descended, Amanda worried about Victoria. What if she came to and found herself sprawled on the marble floor, her clothes in disarray, her hair messed up and her purse open and ransacked. Then she remembered the knife stuck in the door, just about face height.

The doors opened and Amanda rushed out, wild-eyed. She grabbed Manny. "Which floor does she work on?"

"Who…? Oh… she's on the twenty-fourth, but you have to get off on the twenty-second. Where is Ms. Dumas?"

Amanda spun back to the closing door. "Can't explain right now…" The doors closed.

The doors opened on the twenty-second and she rushed toward the reception desk. The two ladies could have been her mother and aunt—kindly, but professional.

"I need Paul, and I need him right now."

The woman on the left pushed a button as the one on the right asked, "Can I ask what this is in regards to?"

Amanda bit down on her tongue that was ready to answer *none of your business*. She thought and then nodded. "My name is Amanda. Tell him there has been an accident and he needs to come to Victoria's right now… and I do mean right now." Turning to the woman on the left, she continued. "That security call button was the wrong thing in this case. Tell them to stand down, and if we need other assistance, it's going to come from 911."

With that, she turned and ran back to the elevator.

The doors opened at the penthouse level and she rushed back into Victoria's apartment. There was no change. Amanda was afraid to touch her as she didn't know if she had done something to set Victoria off.

The door opened and Paul started in and then stared at the knife. Amanda stood and reached over, wiggled and then pulled it free. Sliding it into the boot sheath, she explained. "I hadn't figured out the card thing yet."

He nodded upward. "Ah, to keep the door open..." He stepped over and knelt down next to Victoria. "Vic, it's Paul—can you hear me?"

No response.

Turning to Amanda, he asked, "What happened?"

"We were kissing and... well... it was getting kind of..."

"Hot and heavy?"

Amanda nodded and took a deep breath. "Yeah..." She sighed.

He thought for a moment. "Who was the aggressor?"

"She started it..."

Paul stood. He was calm. "That wasn't the question. Once the kissing became hot and heavy, who was the aggressor? It may be important."

"Me."

"Did you have her pinned down?"

"No... we were standing..."

He nodded, "Against the wall..."

"Yeah."

He stood silent.

Amanda fidgeted. "What?"

"I'm thinking..." He finally looked up. "Did you say anything?"

"No... I don't know... It was kind of... maybe." She ran her fingers through her hair and slumped to one hip. "Yeah, I think I did... something like *finally you're mine...* or something." She looked up almost pleading. "Why?"

He bit his lower lip. "That's what set her off." He turned and started to pick Victoria up. "Help me get her to her bed."

They got Victoria almost standing. Paul knelt and scooped her up like a small child. Amanda had thought of Victoria as a good-sized woman, but in his arms, she looked like a child being carried to bed by her father. She could see in the man love and protection.

Amanda did not know what else to do, so she followed.

Paul laid her on the large bed. In Amanda's head, it should have been a pink four-poster with swags of gauzy fabric or something. Instead, it had a dove-gray leather headboard done in a flat tuck-and-roll style—everything in the room was neutral and styled. Nothing was frilly or girly, but also not masculine, simply tailored. A small glass table and two chairs faced the wall of windows, looking out across the Willamette River and the Ross Island Bridge. It was a million dollar view—and it was in a bedroom that Amanda knew was probably never used for anything more than sleep. The glass table had no dust on it, but she could tell there were no long, lazy breakfasts watching the sun come up or the last light on Mount Hood. This bedroom was all business, and it told Amanda volumes about the woman who slept here. The woman whose lips she could not get out of her head.

"Hi, Karen. It's Paul. Please track down Doctor Nellis and have him come up to Victoria's suite. Thank you."

Amanda turned. "A doctor that makes house calls on a moment's notice?"

Paul hung up the phone softly. "He's the company doctor… he's in the building. We use him for many things, besides being the personal physician for our entire company."

He looked at Victoria resting with her eyes closed. He extended his open hand toward the other room. "Maybe we should…"

They sat in the lounge chairs in what might pass for the living room. The view was of the West Hills. Amanda watched the gondola make its way up to the hospital on the top of Pill Hill. She turned as Paul sat down.

He sighed and rubbed his palms together softly. "How well do you know… I'm sorry. Of course, you don't know much about Victoria."

"I know she doesn't like beer. I know that she has only said *fuck* a couple of times in her life…"

"Make that at least a half dozen times, maybe even a dozen. She even said it in front of polite company once." He looked up and smiled, and then leaned back relaxed. "There was a lot of swearing going on after her mother's funeral."

"That was where you two were?"

He nodded. "Yes, a very small town in a very rural area. You have no idea how provincial. Hell, I had no idea how much of a libertine I was."

Amanda looked at her hands between her legs. "I'm sorry."

"For what?"

"I thought some very… well, harsh things about you and her… but mostly you. I can tell by the way you picked her up that you care for her a great deal."

He studied the young woman. "I think you do, too."

Amanda rolled her eyes and shrugged. "I hardly know her. We met in a dressing room, tried to have a beer, and we kissed a couple of times, and then I called and found out she's flying off somewhere with a dude…"

"That's a lot closer than I've ever been."

Amanda looked at him and frowned.

"We've hugged a couple of times, and we have held each other's hand on occasion… but other than that…"

There was a soft knock on the door. Paul rose and answered it. He took the doctor into the bedroom and explained what had happened.

Paul stopped in the kitchen area. "Can I get you anything to drink? She doesn't keep any food here, but…" He leaned into the refrigerator. Standing, he smiled and cocked his head. "But she does have water." He held up a couple of bottles.

Amanda chuckled as she attempted to lighten the mood. "If you have a little water it would be nice."

"Water it is."

Paul poured the water into glasses and returned. Handing the glass to Amanda, he retook his seat. Amanda got a clear picture of on old woodblock print of Ichabod Crane. The man just did not fit normal-sized furniture.

"How did you and Victoria meet?"

He pointed at the bedroom door. "I think that's at the root of this, and something you need to know. I needed to work my way through college," he continued. "I was almost good enough to get scholarships, but only almost. So I was working nights at the student health clinic. It was usually a great place to get a lot of studying done.

"One Friday night or Saturday morning, Victoria came in. From her clothes, I could see she was one of the *nice* girls." He did air quotes with his two hands. "She was wearing a cashmere sweater over a silk blouse. Her skirt was pleated wool, down to just above her knees. It wasn't an old-fashioned look; but a girl who seriously was there to get a degree so she could start her career. The first thing I noticed was she stumbled, and I looked at her feet—she only had one shoe on. Then I noticed the rumpled look was *actually* rumpled."

Amanda's rounded mouth matched her eyes. "She had been raped..."

He nodded. "She never said a word. She didn't have to. I took her straight back to the doctor's office where there was an old examining table. It was more private. I waited with her while the nurse found the female doctor over at the hospital. I just held her hand. I don't even know if she took my hand or I took hers originally. Now that I think about it, we may have both been in shock. But we sat and waited. It was about an hour. We never talked."

"But you waited with her. You were there for her."

He nodded. "A couple of days later, I saw her in the library. She was hunched over, almost like she expected the universe to start beating her somehow. I couldn't stand it. There was steel in there that had gotten her all the way across the campus. She needed to recognize that. So I sat down and told her that. And I told her that I would always be there for her."

"But not in a girlfriend/boyfriend way..."

"No." He looked at his hands as the palms rubbed back and forth. "I've never... no, not in that way."

"You've never had a girlfriend?"

"No."

"Are you gay? Because I know a nice..."

"No... at least, I don't think so." He leaned back with his water. "I've never had thoughts either way." He shrugged.

They looked up as the doctor came out of the bedroom and quietly closed the door. He set his bag on the counter and then came over and took the third chair. He sunk in almost a slouch. "This is not the way I like starting my mornings, Paul."

"It's not a good way for anyone."

"She started to refocus on where she was, but I helped her relax with a sedative. She should be out until this evening, but I think she shouldn't be alone. I can call the registry and have a day nurse—"

Amanda cut him off. "I'll be here." She pulled out her phone. "I just need your number… and yours, too." She looked at Paul.

Paul liked the newer steady head that was taking care of business instead of a young girl adrift in the crisis. "As long as we're sharing… in fact, I only know your first—"

"Ruddy… with two Ds." She gave both of the men her cell number. "If it goes straight to voicemail, push nine at the beep. It will hang up the call I am on and patch you straight through. If I'm not on the phone, it'll put the phone in alarm mode until I pick it up. I can hear the alarm even when I'm welding—I hacked the volume control."

The doctor promised to check back in about seven that evening and left. The two sat staring into space with their own thoughts.

"Can you hack the speaker so I can hear better?"

"What…?"

He held out his phone. "I'm losing my hearing. I have known it for years. It's the one thing I've never shared with anyone…" His voice dropped. "Not even Victoria."

"Are you sure?"

"I saw a specialist in Switzerland. It is a genetic thing. By the time I'm forty-five, I'll be profoundly deaf. By fifty, I'll be stone deaf. There is no cure—it was the same with my father. He loved to play the violin. In the end, the vibration through his jaw wasn't enough. I had just gone away to college."

Amanda took the phone and worked on it. Finally handing it back, she nodded. He dialed his secretary.

"I can pick up the schedule at the two o'clock point. If you would call down and have them send up a sandwich. In fact, have them send up two lunches here to Ms. Dumas's apartment. Thanks." He listened. "She's resting for now. I'll call Karen next, thanks."

He hung up and then redialed Karen. The conversation was a repeat of the last, and then he hung up.

He looked at the phone and then at Amanda. "Usually I only talk to Karen on my desk phone or in person—so I can watch her lips. Her voice is too soft for me to hear. But I heard her perfectly this time." He jiggled the phone. "Thanks." He set it on the table as he stared at it. Amanda had seen that look in many of the other geeks—four thousand gears were turning, but only half were connecting.

As he looked up, he leaned forward. He gave her an unabashed look from tall boots with knives to the messed-up mop of hair. Finally, he focused on her face. "What is it exactly that you do?"

"In simple terms, I'm a computer programmer."

She thought about the man who still had the factory settings on his smartphone. It had no apps, and the calendar was all but empty. "Have you ever made a paper airplane and thrown it across the room?"

"Sure. What bored kid hasn't?"

"Have you ever seen a jet break the sound barrier?"

"Heard it, but haven't watched it." He was frowning with a question.

She held up a hand. "Do you know what the sound barrier is?"

"It's when the airplane flies faster than the speed of sound."

She put her finger on her nose. "Any idea how fast that is?"

"About five or six hundred miles per hour."

"Close enough. That is Mach 1. It takes a lot of sophisticated engineering to design a plane to do that."

He nodded and shrugged.

"The Space Shuttle at peak moves over the earth about seventeen times faster," she continued.

"Okay…?"

"To say that I am a computer programmer is to say that I make paper airplanes that can fly halfway across this room…" She waved her hand at the living space that consumed a large part of the entire penthouse floor.

Paul snickered. "Better than I ever did."

She smirked kindly. "I'll teach you how to make a killer plane that is so accurate, you can nail someone across the cafeteria."

"Or at a board meeting…?" They both laughed.

Amanda started to continue and then fished up his phone. In seconds, with the help of her smaller and thinner knife, it was in pieces. He didn't seem to care. She held up the SIM card. "The information stored on this card can be changed—so it takes up a lot of room." She took the knife and pointed to a very tiny chip. "That has a hundred times more information in it, but it's fixed and doesn't change. That means it takes up a lot less room. It's called firmware." She held up the SIM card again. "This has software and is random access memory—this is that jet. I am somewhere in that Shuttle.

"Think of that tiny chip as this building. There's a lot going on in here. What I program is basically that oven over there." They both looked up and saw Victoria in the bedroom door.

"That's amazing. I've never seen him focused on anything technical. Paul had a TV once. He could not get the remote to turn it on. He changed the batteries twice before he called me. I went over and plugged the TV into the wall socket."

Paul blushed. "You're supposed to be asleep."

"I must still be. I hear Amanda's voice while thinking she ran away. Then I hear your voice and it does not make sense because you have an all-day meeting with the governor and his people—and Amanda hates you. But I come out here, and here you two are."

Amanda rose and put her hand on Paul's shoulder. "I've got this."

She walked over to Victoria, who slumped against the doorframe. Amanda stopped and they were inches apart. Her voice was soft. "I did run away—but only to get the only help I could think of. I came right back… and I'm here now to stay." She bent over and softly cradled the face with her hands and gently kissed the warm cheek. "I'm here. I'll always be here. But I need you to go get some sleep right now."

"But we need—"

"Not now. We can talk later. We have plenty of time to talk. Right now, sleep. You have the three-day flu, remember?" Amanda reached under Victoria's arm and guided her to the bed. As she stood, Amanda gently removed the white blouse and then the linen skirt. She thought about the pantyhose, bra, and panties, but decided not. She pulled the blankets back and lowered her in. Pulling the blankets back up, she kissed her once on the lips. Victoria was asleep.

Amanda noticed the delivered sandwiches, so she got two more waters as Paul nodded. As she settled back down, she sighed. "She's asleep this time. Where were we?"

He pointed at the kitchen. "The oven."

"Right—so even though it's only a tiny piece of the overall chip, programming it and designing it is somewhere between that jet and the Shuttle. That's what I really do."

"So you write code?"

"That's like driving the city bus on Tenth Avenue. What I do is make sure the light on Northeast Fremont and Forty-Second creates a traffic flow that does not cause problems for Northwest Twenty-Third and Burnside. In addition, I have to consider every vehicle that will drive between those points. The code for the last section of the chip we worked on was a stack of paper twenty-three inches tall."

"Was it a team effort?"

"We're a core of about twenty, but we pull in others as they're needed." She nodded and took a bite. Chewing, she stared at the sandwich.

"Is something wrong?"

She swallowed as she thought about where she was and whom she was eating with. She took a sip of water to clear her mouth, *damn near domesticated*. "The machines at work never spit out something this tasty, is all. It's nothing."

"Dare I ask?" Paul eyebrow rose.

"We get day-old sandwiches at best, week-old pastries—if they could keep them in stock. The best is just plain old cherry flavored Pop Tarts." She took another bite as her eyelids drifted closed in ecstasy.

They ate in quiet and enjoyed the beginning of afternoon sun as it began to creep across the stone floor. The soft quiet was relaxing to Amanda as she could feel the hum of the building, but it was lulling—unlike the tension of the coding chamber.

Paul glanced at his thin gold watch. Amanda wondered if the watch was thicker than a credit card. It was certainly not close to the thickness of her shockproof dive watch.

He rose and cleared the two plates and his glass and water bottle. He toed the trash compactor and shoved it all in. Amanda started to say something about the recyclable bottle but then decided this wasn't the time for a lecture on saving the planet.

Paul looked at the bedroom door and then to Amanda. "I'll be back up, but it'll be probably close to eight or nine. You can pick up the phone and hit the pound sign to get the concierge desk. Tell them whatever you want for dinner and they'll get it delivered." He thought and smiled with the side of his mouth. "Please, just don't order Pop Tarts and energy drinks."

"The key in your pocket has too much access," he went on. "So I'll have one made for you and send it up this afternoon. It'll give you all the access except the office. The IT person will pair it to your cell phone." He thought about what else needed to be covered.

"We'll be fine, Paul."

He nodded with a lost look. "I just..."

Amanda rose and walked to him. She reached up and put her finger on his lips. "Shh... she's in safe hands—I have knives if the zombies break through the outer defenses."

His shoulders relaxed and he smiled. "We've been all

we've had for so long. But I'm glad she found you."

Amanda stepped in, saying, "We don't have time for the bullshit. Just give me a hug and go to work. I'll hold down the fort." She was amazed at how gently he hugged, and then it firmed and she could feel him take and give—what a true hug was about. She started to truly understand the man and the relationship he had with Victoria. There were no shadows in his hug. It was all there.

Finally, he stepped back as his arms and hands dragged along her arms. "Thank you… I guess I've needed that for a long time." He turned and was gone.

The quiet settled around Amanda. She stood thinking about all that had happened. She was energized, yet drained. She walked back to the sun-washed wall of windows. She felt no real heat. Glancing down at the edge of the glass, she realized the windows were triple-pane. The impact was no heat transfer as well as being soundproof.

Sitting on the couch, she slid off her leather jacket and her boots. The boots lay crossed with both knives within easy access. Old habits die hard. She lay back on the couch and was gone by the second breath.

The late afternoon shadow of the tall building two blocks away had started to creep across the marble floor. Amanda felt a weight on her. Her eyes opened with a frown. Wedged between her and the back of the white leather couch was a mass of blond curls on her chest. Victoria's head lay between Amanda's tits as if she were listening to her heartbeat. Amanda wondered how long she'd been there.

Amanda brought her right hand from behind her head and softly stroked the blond curls. It was almost like feeling air or cotton candy. She wondered what Victoria had been like as a little girl—how she had grown up—what kind of person she had been. Her hand softly rested down on the head and petted hesitantly.

Victoria's sleepy voice was soft and drawn. "The leather feels good on my legs, but I think we would be more comfortable in the bedroom… and maybe naked."

Amanda's heart jumped. The images of Victoria's breasts in her bra at the dress shop swam through her mind. Then she realized she hadn't noticed what Victoria was wearing when she had put her to bed—her focus had only been on taking care of her. "I want you to be comfortable."

They lay calm and warm. Amanda wondered if Victoria had fallen back to sleep.

Victoria drew in a deep breath and languidly rose. Her piercing green eyes peeked through the waterfall of curls but looked washed out. Amanda knew she hadn't recovered yet.

They rose. Amanda reached around and under Victoria's arms and supported her as they walked. Victoria's head fell on her shoulder as she snuggled in. Amanda hoped she wouldn't fall asleep before they made it to the bed.

Amanda could feel Victoria fishing her hand to the clasp of her bra. Amanda turned her around and fumbled with the unfamiliar hooks. As she released the straps, she glided her hands slowly forward around to the front, softly cupping the flesh as it fell from the cups of the bra. Amanda bent and kissed the soft neck in front of her. Victoria sagged against her… and then onto the bed.

Amanda finished removing the bra, feeling the soft cups of smooth satin. It felt the way ice cream tasted on a hot summer day. She placed it on the chair where pantyhose were carefully draped over the back. Turning, she took up her legs and carefully tucked them under the sheets. Her hand pressed along the satin sheets. Amanda realized everything about this woman was soft, smooth, and silky—everything she wasn't.

The small voice, the urge to run, lasted for only the span of two heartbeats. She remembered this woman who lay like Sleeping Beauty had tracked her down, not the other way around. For once—not since Samson had offered her a job—she felt wanted.

She swallowed and then swallowed again. The lump was still there.

The voice almost came from nowhere—it was so soft. "I want you naked in here with me." Victoria sleepily rolled to the middle of the bed.

Amanda hesitated for a heartbeat, then her right hand reached the left hem of her T-shirt and she lifted in a large arch—stripping the shirt from her body in one movement. The tight leather pants and her thong were a close second on the floor.

She lifted the sheets and rolled into the waiting arms.

At the last few inches, Amanda slowed down. The connection of lips became a soft landing that languished for seconds. The heat along Amanda's chest rose up along her neck and flushed her cheeks. The urge to roll on top of the woman was strong, but she tempered her need. Amanda lay her head next to hers and placed her hand gently on Victoria's face.

Amanda's finger traced the ridge along the upper lip. The late sun reflected off other buildings and provided a soft gold to the ridgeline. It was exactly the same line; except much larger in the steel and bronze. The artist part of Amanda's mind made a note to polish the ridgeline so the bronze would match Victoria's lips.

15

THE SLEEP HAD done both women a lot of good.

Amanda hadn't realized how much she was burning the candle at more than the obvious two ends until she woke up to find the doctor sitting on the side of the bed. His stethoscope was in his ears and he was listening to Amanda's chest. A soft hand pressed on her right shoulder as her eyes grew large and she stiffened. She looked over at Victoria, who was sitting up wearing some kind of silk T-shirt. Amanda figured it was silk—because she knew it wouldn't be a cotton tank top. Although, in its sheerness and brevity, it covered about as much, or as little, as the tank would have.

"Shh, let him listen. You didn't wake up—he's been here and we've been talking for over twenty minutes."

The doctor moved the stethoscope. "Can you please sit up? I'm going to listen to your lungs through your back."

Amanda folded up and realized that she was wearing a matching shirt to Victoria's. Thank goodness for some privacy. As she sat there, her hand was in her lap and she touched fabric. She looked down at soft pink lace panties.

She didn't know whether to be horrified at the color or laugh at it being so *little girl*. She chuckled softly and smiled shyly up at Victoria.

"Please try to just breathe normally…"

Victoria stifled a laugh.

"Okay, take a few slow very deep breaths."

Finally, the doctor pulled the stethoscope into a fold and stuffed it into his coat pocket. He looked at Victoria. His face was dour. He gently wagged his head.

Victoria lowered her head and looked out from the top of her eyes at the man she had known since he was her family's primary caregiver. "Phillip…" Each letter was delivered as if it was a syllable or separate word of warning.

"I'm afraid it isn't good."

Amanda sat up straight. Victoria braced her hand against her shoulder. They waited.

"Well, my quick evaluation would lean toward prolonged total exhaustion. This combined with a diet consisting of high starchy sugars and copious amounts of caffeine have caused irreparable damage. My conjecture would be a final outcome of death."

He stood somberly. "But youth, being wasted on the young, will probably prolong that outcome well past the prime age of ninety." He finally smiled.

Victoria sank back down into the bed. "Great-aunt Sarah should have just done away with you at birth when she had the chance."

Amanda's head whipped around. "He's a relative?"

Victoria nodded.

"Can I hit him?"

"No bodily harm may be visited on my god-uncle while either is on the premises—you or him." But she gave the man an evil look as she took Amanda's hand and leaned in with a conspiratorial stage whisper. "But that doesn't mean we can't whack him a time or two when he sneaks off to VooDoo Donuts."

The man grew serious. "I was serious about the exhaustion. I don't know what you do, but I can tell that you don't sleep. Victoria will confirm when I arrived, you weren't responsive."

"I don't sleep well."

He pinched at his lips as he looked from Amanda to Victoria and back. "Hmm, maybe a change of venue would do you some good. At least better food than what... Pop Tarts and coffee?"

Amanda lowered her upper eyelids and ground her head around. "Some lawyer has been breaking that lawyer secrets thing..."

Victoria chuckled. "Did you give Paul a dollar?"

"No."

"Well—there you go—you're not a client."

The doctor picked up his bag and nodded. "I'll just leave you two to your dinner. I'll see my way out."

"Good night, Phillip. Thanks again."

"Miss Vic, it is exactly what you pay me a fine living for. I'll be back about nine tomorrow to check up on you. Please don't wake up much before then. I will want to get a urine and blood sample from Amanda." He looked at the horror on her face. "Relax. At least I didn't ask for a stool sample." His laughter carried until the front door closed.

Amanda gazed at Victoria in question.

"No. He was very serious. You didn't make a sound when I dressed you... or the entire time he examined me and we talked."

Amanda pulled the chemise up to expose the pink panties. "But pink?"

"Sorry, my black ones with the little skulls and crossbones were in the wash and I don't own white."

"I've only seen you in a white blouse."

"Exterior clothing only… all of my underwear's in shades that blend with my skin tone."

Amanda huffed. "My tightie-whities blend."

"No, your, umm…" she waved her palm at the thong hanging on the arm of the chair, "is the color next to the little box you mark for ethnic orientation. Your skin tone is more of soft pinkish sand."

"I don't think Target carries that color."

Victoria hummed. "No, I suppose they wouldn't." She stood. "I don't know about you, but I'm starved… and I hope it's not Pop Tarts that I smell." She chortled and lowered an eyelid. "You don't really eat those, do you? I mean, I thought that was a stereotype or some kind of joke…"

"When Hostess went out of business, half of the Silicon Valley prepared to file bankruptcy."

Victoria paused at the door and turned with a frown. "You're serious?"

Amanda nodded as she carefully stood and immediately snuggled into her neck for support. "Serious as a heart attack." The muffled mumble turned into tiny kisses and nibbles along the side of the blonde's neck. As Amanda reached just below the ear, the kisses turned more to sucking as her arm went around the front and softly cupped in an open hand the blonde's right breast. The nipple jumped to attention and she moaned.

Victoria turned and pushed Amanda up against the doorframe as she covered her mouth with her own open one.

Amanda responded as those hands patted the other's body. Slowly, Amanda's leg wedged between the two others and Victoria responded with a gentle grinding ride. Their bodies moved as one except that Amanda moved her upper body to rub more on the larger woman's breasts. Her hard tits moved as massaging hands on the large breasts. All four nipples were hard and responsive to the attention.

Finally, Victoria pulled back, catching her breath. "Wait… I need to… breathe."

Amanda, equally out of breath, laughed softly. "That's what your nose is for."

Victoria leaned into Amanda's neck just below her ear. "No, it is so I can smell you."

"I must stink."

"You smell like new leather."

"I do not, and stop that."

Victoria started to pull back from where she was kissing. Amanda threw her arm up and grabbed the back of the blonde's head pulling it back into her neck. "I didn't say for you to stop right away…"

The two started snickering and any thought of sexual play was put on pause.

They turned toward the rolling cart with the two large chrome domes.

Victoria put her hand out. "Wait."

"What?"

As they faced each other, Victoria thought. Taking Amanda's hand, she pulled her back into the bedroom. She did not lead her to the bed as Amanda had thought—but toward a set of double doors at the end of the room.

Victoria drew open both doors as the large closet was softly illuminated. In the middle, the light intensified to the level of an office. Amanda was stunned by the banks of soft shades of blending. Every color was soft and muted. Nothing was hard or bright in color. Amanda thought about the day she moved into her loft. She had taken a gallon of bright high-gloss red paint and thrown it against the brick wall of used and chipped paint. It was how Amanda lived her life, loud and there. Her bike was fast, loud, and not pretty. Her sculptures were in-your-face and hard edged. Only her computer work showed the finesse she was mentally capable of. And here was a woman she was deeply caring for, who led her life from a place of not being noticed.

Victoria tugged at her hand and dragged her to a large bank of drawers. She started opening two drawers at a time. Amanda could see there were dozens, dozens of panties from solid satin to lace. All of the carefully folded, and arranged panties in each drawer, covered only two or three color values.

Victoria stopped. The back of her finger traced the texture of each pair. Finally, it stopped on one that was a solid panel satin with a small trim of soft tatted lace. She fished them out and turned. Kneeling, she reached up and slid her hands into the tops of the panties in front of her face. She hesitated for only a heartbeat and slid them down. Her hands formed along the outsides of Amanda's legs. Amanda shivered and then stepped out of the pink pair of panties.

Victoria sat looking at the small narrow patch of hair in front of her. She had never seen another woman. She didn't know what she had expected, but the small strip of closely trimmed hair was not it.

"What?"

Victoria shook her head and then leaned forward and kissed the bottom of the patch of hair. Her nose was filled with the scent she had only caught wisps of. The heady embrace was of smells she could detect very softly in Amanda's hair and her neck and when they kissed. She leaned against the woman's crotch and pulled on the clenched butt cheeks. She wanted to be filled with this scent. Then she turned her head and just rested on the other woman. Her arms lay along the skin of Amanda's legs. She could feel the shifting in the taut muscles of the athletic woman. Amanda was much of what she was not... and she wanted to be consumed by that burning lust for life.

Shyly, she rolled back and sat on her heels, adjusting the fresh panties. Without a word, Amanda put her feet through the leg holes and Victoria pulled them up. As she neared the crotch, she stole one more kiss.

As she stood, she reflected the seriousness in Amanda's face. They both knew a next step had been taken—a step of intimacy—and of trust.

Victoria leaned in and kissed Amanda on the cheek as she softly cradled her other with her hand. As she leaned farther to her ear, she whispered. "I saw your hoo-hoo."

The two laughed at the childish name as they danced into the living room.

Dinner was nothing Amanda had experienced before. They moved the cart over to the balcony, and Victoria opened the deck doors. The entire end of the room opened and opened some more as the doors clicked into each other and finally revealed an opening that was twenty feet wide. The closest building that had a view of them was behind the small hedge and a half-mile away. They moved the plates to the table and sat side by side feeding each other off their plates. Amanda didn't know if she had eaten Victoria's food or her own, but between the stolen kisses and the giggles—it didn't matter. The fact that they were in underwear, thirty-six stories above the street also did not matter. The evening was a perfect night for two women to get to know each other on a landing in the middle of the city.

"Does your hair grow that way naturally?"

Amanda picked at her mop of hair with a frown.

"No" Victoria giggled. She nodded her head toward Amanda's lap. "Down there…"

"My landing strip?"

"Landing strip?" Victoria howled, demurely, but howled with laughter. "Is that what you call it?"

"Oh, fuck no. It's just the term for the shape. I guess sometimes you just have to show some people where to land…"

Victoria blushed and shied her head as she mumbled. "Well, it worked… I hope."

Amanda frowned and then realized what had just been said. She tenderly reached over and took Victoria's chin in her hand, turning it toward her. "You had never kissed a woman there before?"

"I've never… I've never been with a woman at all."

Amanda was struck. "So that day in the dressing room… that was your first kiss?"

"Not really. In high school, I kissed another girl."

"And…?"

"Nothing. She slapped me and that was the end of it. She wasn't, we didn't, and it never happened again."

"Not even in college?"

"That was a different fiasco…"

"Paul told me how you two met…"

Victoria thought about it and then reached over and took Amanda's hand. She drew the palm up to her mouth, kissed it long, and with her eyes closed. It was not about passion, it was about pure friendship. She turned the hand over and pulled it to the top of her left breast. "I'm glad you heard it from him. As much as I think of him as my rock, I know there is a very vulnerable side to him. And that event, the event I thought I was over with, still resides inside of his fragile side. My wellbeing is always in that part of him. You might say we are the two sides of a single heart… and I want you to understand that part of me."

"He's your soul mate."

"Hmm," Victoria looked out across the river. "I'm not sure what that is, but I also don't think that comes close to what Paul means to me." She turned and held the hand tighter. "But I also don't want you to see him as an obstacle because he's not."

"I think he and I reached an understanding today. You won't have to worry."

Victoria kissed Amanda's hand again and let it go. The hand reached around and pulled on the shoulder. The kiss as warm and gentle—the heat and power of desperation was gone. There was just a gentle softness that was reassuring.

The kiss ended with them holding their foreheads together. They were looking through the tops of their eyes. The green was more vibrant now, and the deep brown reflected the stars or other night lights. "Maybe we can go inside now?" Amanda nodded, causing the two heads to nod. They both snickered.

As they stood, Amanda took up her dishes and then looked at Victoria, who was standing there perplexed.

"What? Don't we clear our plates?"

Victoria stopped… thinking.

"I don't know… I've never eaten out here before."

Amanda was stunned. She threw her hands up at the night view over the river, the bridges, and the city. "All of this... and never?"

The older woman shook her head. "Never. I have never had a reason to. Other than the occasional breakfast sent up... I've never had a reason to eat here."

"Where do you eat?"

"Most of the time—at the office while I or we work."

Amanda put her hands on her hips. "Let me get this straight... you work your ass off but then never take the time to enjoy what you are working so hard for. Doesn't that seem a little nutso to you?"

Victoria smiled shyly. "Well, I never thought about it in those terms."

"So you were just working on a fat bank account..."

"I was just working."

In her exasperation, Amanda became distracted as she realized her hands kept feeling the smooth fabric of her panties. She blushed.

Victoria moved in closer. "What just went through your mind? Because you are blushing big time... and your nipples..."

"I just realized that I was feeling myself up... These panties feel... sexy. And this T-shirt is amazing. It's either chillier than I think out here or it's this T-shirt because my nips are hard as rocks right now."

"I noticed... and I was hoping it was me. And it's called a chemise."

"My hard nipples?"

Victoria moved closer and her flat hand glided up Amanda's firm body, under the chemise, as she raised it above the hard nipples. "No, the shirt is a chemise. The hard nipples are called…" she leaned over and kissed into a soft suck, "exciting."

Amanda moaned softly as the electricity raced through every part of her body on the way to the nipple being licked and sucked. She was frozen in place, unable to respond, just to receive. "Oh, my God. That is amazing." Her fingers laced into the curls as she urged the woman not to stop.

Victoria nibbled, sucked and kissed her way up from the firm breasts as her hands took over. As she stood, she stepped behind Amanda and leaned over into the exposed neck as she continued to rub and smooth the sides of her breasts. Victoria's lips took tiny lip nibbles along the neck as she made her way to the lobe of the ear. Under the light of the stars, she nibbled and moaned, "I want to be yours…"

Amanda turned and the embrace was simple, gentle and giving. Nothing needed saying. They just danced the dance of the hug as the moon rose over Mount Hood.

Amanda held her by the shoulders—but close enough for them to rest their foreheads on the other. "We'll work through all of this and anything else that comes up."

"There is so much I want to do… but I don't know what or how…"

Amanda folded her into a hug. "Shh… It's going to work out. Everyone has to learn things at the right time. A wise woman once told me *'if you came to a relationship complete, then why did the last one end?'*"

Victoria laid her head on Amanda's shoulder as they stood there. It just seemed so natural. But finally, she drew back.

Amanda chuckled. "That cold air must be going around…" She pointed at the four hard nipples.

Victoria, embarrassed at first then started to laugh.

"I've always been embarrassed when my nipples get hard. In college, I used to put Band-Aids on them if it was going to be the least bit chilly." She smiled shyly as she looked into Amanda's eyes and saw the same memories. "But you make me feel like I should be proud of them…"

Amanda lifted Victoria's chemise and looked at the darker pink and larger nipples than she was used to seeing in the mirror. "Oh, baby… you have a lot to be proud of." They laughed.

Victoria pulled the top down. "Stop that." She had a thought and grabbed Amanda's hand to pull her through the penthouse and through her bedroom toward the large bathroom. "There is one other thing I have never used… because I could not figure out how to turn it on."

She opened a small glass door onto a small private balcony the size of an office or standard master bedroom—in the corner stood a covered hot tub spa. She turned and snuggled into Amanda's arm and side. Resting her head on the shoulder, she softened her voice to that of a begging child. "Can Mandi turn it on for us?"

"I don't know if it has nipples to make hard, but I know I want hot water… and you naked." She stepped forward and pulled back the lid. The water was hot, and the digital readout said it was one-hundred and two degrees. She examined the buttons and then turned. "Did you want it to make noise?"

The nude woman stepped over and pulled at Amanda's chemise. "I don't care… I just want you naked and in there with me."

16

THE SHEETS AND blankets had fallen off and been replaced a few times during the night. The two found they squirmed just like puppies sleeping in a pile. Victoria felt a slight chill and bent down to pull up the last of the wandering blankets. She stopped halfway and softly kissed the dimple in the butt cheek Amanda presented to her. She blushed in the dark at having become so brazen about another person's body.

She drew up the blanket and covered them as she snuggled into Amanda's back. The other moaned contentedly and snuggled back into the larger spoon. Victoria gently nuzzled in the curve of Amanda's neck behind her ear. The scent of her was strongest there. It had the raw spice of her skin and hair. Victoria took a deep, slow smell. She did not want to exhale. The scent was better than any food she had ever remembered eating. She drew another slow breath.

Amanda snickered softly. "That tickles. But don't stop."

Victoria wiggled her body slightly, grinding her crotch

against the naked butt. The extra contact was gently electric. Victoria took another breath. "I think you had an orgasm last night…"

A hand slid out of the blanket with two fingers extended.

"I'm jealous."

There was a calm pause and then Amanda rolled over gently—breaking the nested spoons. She looked deeply into the green eyes. She studied the area around the eyes, down the nose and resisted kissing the ridgeline that consumed Amanda. "You were close, and then it's like a switch is thrown and you stopped…"

Victoria knew that they were on very personal territory here. It was not so much about the subject matter as it was about trust. The kind of trust she almost had with Paul. For Victoria, it was the very definition of scary territory. "That… that's the way…" She froze.

Amanda stroked the curls and the side of her face. "The way it always is?"

Victoria nodded as she buried herself into Amanda's chest—her ear between the small breasts, the heartbeat pounding softly. Her shoulder found the hollow of Amanda's armpit and she snuggled in. She retreated.

Amanda let her rest for a few minutes. She knew she wasn't sleeping. She stroked the blonde curls and then let her hand rest on Victoria's shoulder. She had never felt as completely secure as with this bundle of two intertwined bodies. Not even with…

She remembered Jody.

"Do you have a handheld mirror?"

There was a stop in the rhythmic breathing and then a slight nod. "Why?"

"Because it's about time... Where is it?"

"It's in the bathroom... somewhere."

"Good." Amanda slid out. "Because I need to pee anyway."

Victoria sat up and then smiled mischievously. "Fuck... okay, I'll use the guest toilet." They both snickered at how comfortable Victoria had become about the word.

Victoria entered and frowned. The mirror lay on the bed where Amanda had pulled off the blankets and top sheet. The pillows were piled at the headboard. Amanda was trying to figure out the sheer drapes.

"What are you looking for?"

"How to open the drapes."

Victoria laughed. "For a nerd, you are some kind of Luddite." She touched one of the switches on the panel along the wall by the door. The drapes in front of Amanda started to draw open. She touched two more and the others opened as well.

Amanda watched them open with her arms held spread. Victoria admired the strong ropes of muscle that ran down her back and tightened the buttocks. The legs were smooth cylinders of muscle ending at small feet. Victoria most admired that she unabashedly stood to face a quarter of a million people—exposing her privates. Victoria laughed softly.

Amanda turned with a huge smile. "What?"

The blonde giggled. "They can all see your hoo-hoo."

Amanda smiled as she walked to the bed and sat with her leg under her. "The four hundred foot elevation over the general altitude of Portland creates a refraction ratio of seven to one. All anyone would be able to see, if this were just standard glass, would be the reflection of the sky. But I've seen this building many times before from that hill and know that there is a mirrored low-energy coating or film on the outside of the glass that triples the sum of the ratio."

Victoria sighed. "You make me feel like a Luddite."

Amanda frowned at the woman who was slowly crawling across the bed to her. "How do you even know what a Luddite is?"

Victoria kissed her with a soft touch. "Miller vs. Ford, 1909. It was a case of the automobile disrupting the tranquility of life in the small town of Torrance, Ohio. And you are so sexy when you talk that geek stuff."

Amanda gave her a quick pecking kiss as she laid back. "Who won?"

"The future—the judge found Mr. Miller to be a Luddite and a rejectionist to anything modern. Except that the council for Ford Motor Company had discovered the man had a secret telephone installed in his kitchen pantry. There was some competition between three towns for a new railroad, and Mr. Miller was a major landholder that would gather a huge windfall should the township be chosen for the new rail line. He was scared that if cars were to become common, the need for a railroad would become obsolete."

Amanda lay there, admiring her. "Talk about nasty sexy talk… wow. And this stuff just rattles around in that pretty head of yours?"

"It was the first case in Civil Law that tested the quality of life issue. You might say that is my oven that I bake in— in this building."

"Cars against people?"

"No, I help companies stay within certain bounds so they don't have to waste time and money defending themselves from stepping on toes. It saves them money and effort in the long run, but also makes them look better in the public eye. I help them be a better neighbor."

"Well, it's still sexy listening to you talk dirty that way...." She smiled and kissed her knee. She ran her tongue around to the inside of the knee as she gently pulled it away from the other leg. Victoria passively slid down on the pile of pillows. Amanda stopped her. She reached up and pulled her panties off, but stopped Victoria's progress to become prone. She kissed and licked her way toward Victoria's upper leg. She could feel the shivers of anticipation. As she finally reached Victoria's crotch, she reached around behind her and grabbed the mirror. She brought the mirror to her chest as she rose up on her elbows.

"Show me how you masturbate."

She watched as the tiny pale freckles from bellybutton to face disappeared in a single flush of red. It confirmed what Amanda had gathered the night before. "Have you ever masturbated?"

"I've never even said the word!"

"Not even during a soapy shower?"

"I've kind of, well... washed myself a bit extra... It felt good for a while, but then it just started to irritate and then after... college."

Amanda put out her hand and laid it on the woman's crotch. It just rested there, in reassurance. "Hey, hey... we're looking forward here. We're just moving into new territory."

Victoria smiled in a side drawn smirk. "Where no man has gone before..."

Amanda frowned and then laughed as she caught the Star Trek reference. "Who would have ever guessed that you were a closet lipstick nerd?"

"Lipstick?"

Amanda cleared her throat. "We'll get back to that."

One step at a time. She pulled out the mirror and held it up. "This is where you start. Biology 101 had bad charts with nothing that really helped in the real world. I know—I aced it and still had a lot to learn that summer with Jody."

"Who's Jody?" Amanda could hear the jealousy in the question.

"We'll get to her later." She thought a moment and offered up a silent thank you. Jody had shown her about her body but had also been the role model for teaching someone else. "For right now, just say '*Thank you, Jody.*'"

Victoria watched the woman between her legs. She also was looking for the first time at her own pussy. "Thank you, Jody. I think I want to meet this person."

Amanda smiled. "You have no idea."

Victoria's line of sight was drawn back to herself. Amanda could tell she was fascinated. She guided Victoria's left hand to lie on the fur patch with the fingers extended over the lips. "Using your first and second fingers, push and spread the lips like this." She guided the spreading of the upper part and exposing the important small bump.

Gently, Amanda slid her one hand up and spread her first finger and thumb. She placed her thumb on Victoria's anus, and the finger well into her pubic hair. "Everything here is your vulva. Some people think it is their vagina because of that stupid side cut picture was drawn by some dude in Cincinnati or Calcutta. Just remember that dudes are ignorant about this stuff." She looked up.

Victoria was nodding slowly with a shy smile on her face. Amanda guessed this was news to her, too.

Much later in the final calm, Amanda slid up along Victoria's backside and curled in. She nuzzled into the wet curls and smelled the heat and scent of the other woman. Smiling, she kissed the back arch of Victoria's ear and rewarded by more spasms rippling through her body. She slid her hand down between her legs and rubbed herself for a small release. As she stiffened in her release, her body shook and Victoria stiffened.

Rolling over, Victoria looked at her with a frown. "Did you just have an orgasm?"

Amanda smiled shyly. "Yes, a little one… but I left the big one for you later."

Victoria's mouth opened in aghast. And then she started laughing weakly. "I have something that should make the news as a 7.4 on the Richter scale, and you just rubbed out a little one?"

Amanda nodded. "If I had touched myself while I was licking you, I would have exploded, too. But then, you wouldn't have known it. When I come like that with or for you—I want you to know it was because of you. I want you to know it, and take pleasure in it. When you masturbate, it's all about you and your fantasies, but when you make love to someone, it's about the two of you or the one on the receiving end."

"Was this another bit of wisdom from the wise Jody?"

"No, this was from my boss, Samson… but he didn't exactly put it that way." She smiled. "It had to do with killing people."

"Killing people?" The image of the two knives flashed through her mind.

"It's a Dungeons & Dragons thing—not about real life. Although Samson says the philosophies of the game carry over into real life. It's about living in a space that respects others."

"He sounds like a wise man."

"Oh, I'm guessing he is a very wise man—I think he got that philosophy stuff from his wife, Tosika."

"He's married to a Japanese woman? He must be very special, as well."

Amanda tipped her head, "Why?"

"They are known to be very picky about marrying a white man."

Amanda laughed. "White? Not very likely—try Irish-Samoan-Japanese-Hawaiian."

"Wait… who do you work for?"

"Big I."

"We have a contract with them. They provide…well…" She laughed. "Ordinarily, I would say computer stuff… but with you… fuck. I'm out of my league."

The muted sound of Darth Vader's Imperial March echoed through the apartment.

"Shit." Amanda sprang up and raced into the living room.

Victoria followed to find her racing around. "What are you…?"

"My pants…"

"They're in the closet—I hung them up."

Amanda stopped and blinked. "You hung up leather?"

"Of course, silly… or it might wrinkle…?" Victoria blinked once. "Fuck. It doesn't wrinkle, does it?"

Amanda grabbed her head and kissed her hard on the lips. "I love you. There's so much to learn." She raced into the bedroom.

A moment later, she walked out of the closet talking on her cell phone. Victoria lounged in one of the easy chairs looking out over the city. Amanda glanced at the other chair, and instead, sat on Victoria's lap. The two wiggled around and fit snugly in the large chair.

"Paul? Yeah, I know a Paul…"

Victoria could hear a deep rumble that may have been a volcano, an earthquake or a voice. She mouthed to Amanda. *Is that Samson?* Amanda nodded. Victoria put out her hand for the phone.

"Hello, Samson? This is Victoria Dumas. We've met a few times when you've visited. What does Paul need?" She listened. "Can she do that?" She nodded, and then pinched the bridge of her nose. "Then are we being sent either a very valuable person, such as yourself, or someone of lesser quality than our contract calls for?"

She smiled at Amanda and put her hand on her thigh. Playfully, she quietly probed near the small landing patch. Amanda snickered silently, and with a mock stern face, slapped her hand—but didn't move it.

"I understand the security levels and all of that, but my question still stands. Is there a problem with Amanda taking care of our needs? After all, she is here now."

Amanda watched the woman smirk as she pointed at the corner of the room three feet away. *She has Samson backed into a corner.*

"So, if our loss prevention officer can get her the needed clearance, she can take over our contract?" She looked up and smiled. "Yes, I think what Paul may be talking about would have her in-house for more than a few hours— probably a few days. I guess we'll know better once we have a meeting with Paul, loss prevention, and our in-house IT department."

She listened to the man admit defeat. "Very nice talking to you again too, and please, call me Victoria—Amanda does. Goodbye."

She handed the phone back to Amanda with a smile. "It looks like you are to be our new in-house liaison."

Amanda stared at her. "My gawd… that was the sexiest phone conversation I've ever heard. That man is a force of nature."

"Yes, but a force of nature that understands where his paycheck comes from."

"What was the part about security clearance?"

"Have you ever been arrested? Do you harbor ill will toward the government of the United States? Do you have any terrorist leanings or friends? How many speeding tickets have you racked up on the mean machine?"

Amanda sat stunned and trying to remember the questions. She realized how completely their relationship had flipped. She was now the less assertive. "I haven't been caught, I don't know anyone enough to hate them, the terrorist that I know are in dungeons and running from dragons…"

"Tickets?"

"The day you were supposed to be back."

"How bad?"

"If you were a squirrel in Forest Park, you would probably call me a terrorist. He wanted to write me for splitting the lanes for the last few years, but all he witnessed was my riding on the footpath."

"So a clean record?"

"I don't know if I should be insulted, embarrassed, or proud." She nodded.

"Today, just be glad and proud. We'll get the ball rolling right after breakfast."

Amanda raised her arm and sniffed herself. "I think a shower is the first thing."

"It's a big shower."

"Yeah, I guess taking a bath in the hot tub would be a little bit over the top." They laughed like little girls as they played grab ass into the bathroom. Amanda missed the text message from Samson. *Lucy, you have some 'splaining to do.*

17

AMANDA STOOD WITH the welding goggles pushed back on her head. The last bit of brazing was done. The ridgeline, she sanded to 30,000-grit with micro emery cloth and then got out the electric polishing tool and toothpaste. The lip ridge was a golden mirror. She had passed the orbital sander over the whole face until it was down to smooth and no catches and then ran a double thick body disk over it all to polish the highlights.

She pulled the mask up over her nose and pulled the clear goggles down. She reached in and pulled one of the cans from the shaker. She turned the small white nozzle to the vertical fan pattern and began to apply the clear coat that would prevent oxidation of the bronze or rusting of any steel that she had missed.

The inside of the face was a smooth matte black. The vinyl print that matched her helmet lay on the large table inside the building. Amanda had moved the painting out into the driveway. She didn't want the smell to linger in the loft that evening when Victoria came over for dinner.

Friday had been a lost day with her head in a large complex computer system that she needed to learn. It was going to take a lot more days to feel comfortable with the system as it was—before she could make any recommendations about any changes.

As they had leaned against the wall of the elevator, Victoria mentioned she wanted to see where Amanda lived… not just the driveway. Amanda had nodded sure and then panicked—the place was a mess and the face wasn't done. She begged for the weekend.

Saturday she had swept and mopped the floor after dusting everything in the two-thousand square feet of space. She knew it was her white cotton tank top compared to Victoria's satin chemise, but it was who she was and where she lived.

She had tack-welded together a bed frame that at least got the futon up off of the floor. If she had time, she was thinking about a copper headboard out of the foot-square plates she had picked up a few years ago for the purpose but had put it off until now.

In the light of the early morning, she finished the paint and pulled the trolley back inside and closed the door. The smell would be what it would be. There was only so much she could do.

The buzzer rang at the front. Amanda frowned. *What the hell did Sam want?*

"Fuck you, Sam." She jerked the door open to find Victoria standing there.

The woman smiled. "Okay, if that's what you want…"

"What're you doing here? You weren't coming until six tonight." She looked behind her into the loft, scared.

"Do you have someone else in there?"

Amanda's head snapped around. "No. Fuck, no."

"Are you going to invite me in?"

Amanda paused. "Oh, that is a definite fuck no. The place is still a mess, I'm a mess, and…"

Victoria stepped up to her lover and grasped the mop of hair between the particle mask and the welding goggles. She drew her close and took a deep smell before she buried her mouth in Amanda's. The scent in Victoria's nose was of work—burned steel, smoke, and a pungent, earthy scent. Amanda almost smelled like great sex—or what Victoria imagined great sex was going to smell like with Amanda in her place.

As Amanda finally pulled back, catching her breath, Victoria explained. "I don't want a prissy cleaned-up place—I live in one. One is enough for us. I want to know what makes you smell so sexy and earthy like the air in Forest Park just after a summer rain. I want you, just you, just the way you are." She waved at Amanda's garb. "The cotton shirt, the leather pants. If that's who you are, and who you want to be, then that's what I want. If I wanted a clone of me, there are four women in the office who would qualify. But that isn't you. I've made my choice…"

Amanda stepped back, and as she reached out, muttered, "Oh, shut the fuck up. I don't have time for your bullshit—just kiss me."

As they tried to suck the other's tongue from their heads without choking on their laughter, they heard a throat clearing behind them.

Amanda spoke into Victoria's mouth, "Fuck you, Sam. I'm busy here."

"Tell her that…"

Amanda looked up to see her long-time friend holding

his phone out to Amanda. "Oh, fuck…" She took the phone.

"What..?" She listened.

"So… I tried on a dress. There is no fucking way I'm wearing that kind of shit. So you being down a dude doesn't make it unbalanced… means that I'm off the hook." She took a breath as she listened.

"No, you don't get it. I'm not coming."

Victoria gave her a stern look with her hand out. Amanda gave her the phone. "Hello, Amanda lied. She *will* be there and you have a person for each side. We'll see you then." Her thumb hung up the phone. She turned around and handed it to Sam. "Thank you, but we're done here."

He knew when he had just been dismissed. He turned and walked back into his door and softly closed it.

Victoria looked at Amanda. "I just saved your ass, so now you're mine. Grab whatever you think you need for the day and come on."

"But I'm filthy…" She frowned. "Where are we going?"

"I'm not going to ask you if you love me… yet. But do you ever want to have sex with me again?"

"Well, duh?"

"Then you will be sitting in my car, with your hand up my skirt, and kissing me in less than two minutes. Because, in one hundred and twenty seconds, I will drive off. If you are not there—it will be forever."

Amanda blinked and thought. She pulled the goggles, mask, and leather apron off. With a heave, she threw them in the door. The door swung shut as her hand was feeling low on the skirt where the butt tucked in at the legs. "I like when you talk dirty like that. It is sooooo sexy." She leaned over and kissed Victoria on the ear.

Victoria giggled as the tiny kiss was ticklish.

Victoria kept Amanda's left hand trapped between her legs as she drove up into the lower hills and a ritzier neighborhood. The Pearl and Northwest 23rd were for the newly rich and the wannabe rich. This neighborhood, with its streets grandly shaded with the drape of old tree, softly whispered old money. Amanda watched the perfectly landscaped gardens embracing the exquisitely painted Victorian homes, as they silently slid by. She never even knew this kind of neighborhood existed in Portland.

Several minutes later, they sat on small pine stools. They dipped huge sea sponges into wooden buckets full of soapsuds. They lathered each other down.

Victoria moaned as Amanda ran two soapy sponges over her back, shoulders and then over her breasts. "I need to get some of these stools and buckets for my place."

Amanda kissed her soapy neck. "Not many places have a shower area like this."

Amanda kissed her way to Victoria's earlobe and nibbled. "When I built my shower, I had scored two shipping pallets of granite tiles. I laid them out and then kept laying them out until they were all used. I think you could wash your car in my shower—it's where I wash my bike."

Victoria looked up with a wry smile. "Now there is an image to wet the..." She frowned.

"Pussy?"

"It just sounds so..."

"Crude? Vulgar? Unrefined?"

"In that neighborhood."

"I don't think you go to high tea and talk about things that make your pussy wet." They both snorted, and Victoria squeezed the sponge as she flung the water over her shoulder at Amanda.

As they slipped into the hot Japanese-style bath, Amanda grew curious. "So you don't have time to eat on your veranda, you don't have time for relationships, you don't seem to do anything but work. So how did you find this place?"

Victoria melted until her head rested on the edge of the tub. "You know the redhead that met us and let us in?"

"She's the owner?"

"More than that—she owns half of this and the next block. My hairdresser owns the other half. You'll meet Freddie later. Now, hush and relax, or you won't enjoy what comes next."

"Are you going to eat me?"

"Don't be vulgar with your impatience—that's later. Shh." The two snorts were soft and turned into low moans as the hot water did its magic.

The small Asian woman was back. "Your tables are ready..."

As they lay on the massage tables, the smaller hands worked on Amanda's back. "You have very hard muscles in your back. I think you need a big man. Hans, you switch with me. You make her relax." The Asian woman leaned in close to Amanda's ear. "If my husband touch you wrong, you tell me—I beat him for being bad boy when we get home." Amanda chuckled.

The man came over and started along the spine. Amanda could feel the difference immediately. She groaned. "Why have I never had a massage before?"

Hans chuckled. It was a rumbling sound of bowling balls in a rack. "Because you were waiting for me... Tan was right, you are nothing but steel bars back here. What do you do?"

"I'm a computer programmer."

"Not with these muscles, and this doesn't come in a gym either."

"I sculpt metal and ride a motorcycle..."

"Hmm, push the handle bar on the side you want to turn into. It doesn't take much, but it will stop you having this muscle bunch up and ache." He pushed on the bulge just above her butt.

She shrieked.

"Ya, see? Hans knows these things."

As the massage ended and Hans left, Amanda started to get up. A gentle hand pushed her back down. Janice's cloud of red hair floated down next to her head. "You're not done yet."

If anyone had ever told Amanda that she could almost have an orgasm by having her face rubbed with goo, she would have laughed. She took a deep breath and let out an almost moan. From somewhere close, she could hear Victoria's voice. "It's certainly got to be better than a lunch of Pop Tarts and energy drinks..."

Amanda started to respond with a *fuck yeah* but considered where she was. "It most certainly is."

Victoria laughed. "Was that a fuck yeah that I heard?" All four women laughed.

Finally, the redhead peeled Amanda up off of the bed she had been reclining on for two hours of massage and facial heaven. "I'm Janice, by the way." She presented a tall glass of water with lime and a cucumber slice floating in it. "Here, drink it all. You need to replenish your electrolytes and water. You'll get three more of these glasses while Freddie takes care of you." She turned. "When you're ready, your changing room is through this door."

Victoria was sitting with her eyes closed. "Janice? Is Freddie waiting?"

The redhead stopped in the doorway and turned. "He's just finishing up with another special. Billy just got here, so take your time. You know Billy's no good until she has at least half of that quad-shot in her."

Amanda followed Victoria down the hallway that connected the spa to the most exclusive salon in the city. If you did not have Freddie's private cell phone number, and he yours—you were not being seen.

As they walked out into a solarium of soft light and two chairs, a flamboyant man accosted Victoria. Towering more than a foot over her, he wrapped himself around her and cooed and made yummy noises—until he saw Amanda.

Amanda did not know if he had seen the leather, the knives, or the dirty white tank top, but for some reason, she was certain he had reacted to her hair instead.

He squeaked and hid behind Victoria. "Ah Chihuahua, someone's following you, and I don't know if it's a zombie or something from the river!" He sounded like a Hollywood snake with a bad lisp. Amanda almost laughed but still considered pulling a knife.

Victoria growled. "Freddie, if you don't behave, I'll take my business elsewhere. All of it."

"Oh, gawd, Vicky… lighten up, girl. Freddie's allowed at least a little fun on Sunday." He moved in a fluid motion around Victoria as he held his index finger on the top of her head.

"This is Amanda."

The large man stuck his right hand out. He introduced himself in a deep, husky voice. "My real name is John… but people seem to have a hard time with such an exotic name, so I just go by Freddie. Everything from here on is for show or my artistic, creative nature coming out. I don't know which." He spun and his hip shot out as he pranced away with his hands held out, bouncing with each step. "You be the judge and tell me in a few years."

Amanda did laugh. "Okay, I'm in." She fell into Victoria's arms, laughing. She mouthed the question with a frown, *where did you find him?*

Victoria mouthed back *I kept him out of jail for murder.*

"Over here, cupcake," he sang, patting the pink chair.

As Amanda settled in, the man stood behind her and they both looked in the mirror. His fingers combed her mop and then he shoved them up and grabbed both sides of the hair and pulled gently. He repeated the process a few more times and then raked the top and sides as he drew the hair back. He flopped his head over to one side and gazed at the side of Amanda's head. "Hmm, cute ears... Victoria, my sugar dumpling, did you happen to notice these cute ears?"

"Don't nibble on them, Freddie. They're very sensitive—and they're exclusively mine."

He snaked his upper body around so he was looking into Amanda's face while still holding his fingers in her hair. "How does she ever know that they are sssensssitive?" His eyes went large, and he smiled as he wiggled his eyebrows. He snapped back around behind Amanda and stage-whispered in her ear. "And she is such a bitch not to share."

He stood and called out. "Billy, stop getting stoned on the Tanzania Peaberry and come out here for a moment."

The woman who stepped out of the back room was not what Amanda would have ever thought would be named Billy. She could have been a close cousin to Tosika. She was short to Freddie's tall, and tiny and thin. She did not walk—

she glided. She was direct and climbed onto Amanda's knees and straddled her lap. It put their faces almost at equal heights. Amanda had never had her personal space so invaded.

Billy's eyes examined almost every hair. Amanda felt that she was ignored to the point of only being a wig stand for her hair.

Billy leaned in as she pulled and felt the nature of the hair before her. "Nice set of knives… Kershaw or Gerber?"

Amanda wasn't sure if she had heard right. "They were custom made for me by a guy named Tim Whitesides. He studied under Jody Sansome and Dale Hauss."

"Dale Hauss… Katana fold or Damascus steel?" Her hands and examination never paused or wavered.

"One of each. The thinner dirk is Damascus."

The woman slid off of Amanda's lap. She pointed up and down. "This is what you wear all the time. What kind of motorcycle?"

"Yamaha V-Max… milled to twenty over."

"Ever get it over one-fifty?"

"One thirty-eight." Amanda wasn't sure if she was interviewing for a job or this woman was hitting on her.

Billy turned to Freddie. She pinched her upper lip together with her fingers as she thought. "Remember that movie in the late seventies? I think it was Shirley McClain."

The tall man looked toward the ceiling. "Killed a bunch... No that was... Oh, yes… The short shag."

Billy pointed at him with a finger gun and dropped her thumb as the hammer. "Bingo." She turned toward Amanda. "You don't want it too short or with those tits and the tank top it screams dyke. You want a statement that is softer, more baby dyke but says I just took my helmet off, and if you don't like it, I can provide some steel through your heart."

Amanda was shocked and looked at a smiling Victoria. Victoria shrugged and pursed her lips, nodding in agreement. "I would say that about sums you up. But what is a baby dyke?"

Billy gave her a hard stare and then turned to Amanda. The blank look confirmed that neither was deeply vested in the community. She turned back to Victoria but waved her hand up and down at Amanda. "Basically, it's a tight, slim, muscular young lesbian. Tuff as nails, but still has a soft inside—tender like a baby."

Victoria nodded slowly, and the green eyes caught on the brown ones in the chair. Her smile grew and Amanda was drawn in. *Who cared about title beyond girlfriend and lover?*

Freddie flounced over and pulled Amanda out of the chair. "Shampoo time," and dragged her off to the wash as Billy rolled a small table over toward Victoria.

The hour flew by, and finally, Freddie spritzed down Amanda's hair until it was soaked and hanging. "Okay, I'm done." He bent down so that his face was next to Amanda's as he turned her to the mirror. "Absolute virtuosity." He smiled. He laughed. "Of course, you don't see it. I said I'm done. You, on the other hand, have just stepped from the shower." He handed her a large towel.

"Dry it roughly." She did.

"Now use the ends of the towel and get the rest of the wet out. You want to just leave it damp."

He watched and then felt. "Great. Now run your fingers through front to back. Good. And now run your fingers up slowly past your ears. You need to grab all of that hair… and pull it straight out away from your head."

The hair started to resemble Bozo the Clown.

"Now the back—just the same way. Great and now scrunch it all up like this." He grabbed large handfuls and made fists. She repeated the action. "All over, my lump of sugar, all over."

Billy left Victoria's nails and wandered over to Amanda. "Perfect. Now shake your head like a wet dog just coming out of the river."

Amanda shook until she felt her brain rattle. As her eyesight cleared, she was looking at a perfect shag haircut that sculpted to her head and layered with enough loft to have some feminine poof. The mop she had known since high school was gone. She had gone from bad girl to woman in a matter of minutes.

"Oh, my God."

Amanda thought it was Victoria who had spoken, but she looked in the mirror to see Janice standing next to Freddie. She had her arm around her tall brother. "Freddie, that is amazing."

His voice was hushed and reverent. "Not me, sweet thang, this is all Billy. She can see what is inside of a person and pull it out. I jus' nail it to the wall so it quits wiggling."

Amanda watched in the mirror as Victoria slowly got up and walked around her silently. Amanda could not read her face. She watched her with a worried look. She was afraid Victoria wouldn't like the new look. It would take months to grow her mop back out to what it was. All of her fears began to boil in her stomach.

Victoria finally circled and stepped to the side of the chair. She leaned in, her lips hovering close to Amanda's ear. Her breath was hot on the still damp hair. She whispered with only her breath, "Don't touch me, or I will come right here." She leaned her head against Amanda's. In the mirror, Amanda could see that her eyes closed as the woman fought for control.

After a minute or so, Amanda saw Billy come around to look at her from the front. She was smiling at the two heads together. Amanda softly smiled. "I guess we'll take it."

18

IN THE LEXUS, the two sat quietly considering what had just happened. Victoria turned to ask, and Amanda was right there. Her mouth was wet and all over Victoria's. Soon, Amanda's fingers were in her hair as she pulled the blonde's head closer so she could nuzzle and kiss her neck from the jaw to the ear.

Victoria hesitantly placed the tips of her fingers in Amanda's new haircut. Amanda grabbed her hand and jammed it into her hair. That was the only permission Victoria needed. The no muss hair became mussed as the kissing heated up. If it had been winter, the windows would have fogged over—but it was summer and people still walked by in the street.

Amanda opened her eyes to look at her lover's face. Out of the corner of her eye, she saw a woman across the street gawking at the two women making out in the car. She started to snicker. Victoria's eyes opened and looked at her, then across the street. She laughed. "Give her the finger for me." This set them both off again.

Victoria gained some control and fumbled for the keys in the ignition. Amanda reached under her arm to cup her breast and realized Victoria had no bra on. The nipple in her palm was a hard little pebble. Amanda knew what it looked like and how it tasted. She became wet as she focused on the slow rotation she performed on the nipple. Victoria leaned back. Her breathing was short—almost panting. "You have to stop that or we'll get arrested for what I want to do to you. I need to drive."

She started the car and they drove off, laughing like maniacs.

"Pull into the alley. I'll go around and open it up." Amanda jumped out.

Victoria closed her eyes as she slowly massaged her breasts through the pale sand-colored satin. She had felt so naughty by not wearing a bra and had been afraid everyone could tell. But once she saw Amanda, she didn't care anymore. Now she was glad she had dared to let her nipples rub on the satin and be available for her lover's caresses. Her left hand lay in her lap and she pulled her skirt up.

Suddenly, she opened her eyes and looked around. She was in the alley, and nobody could see what she was doing. She looked around for cameras and seeing none, she relaxed.

She laid her head back and her eyes closed halfway with the pleasure her fingers gave the two parts of her body through the satin of the shirt and the satin of her panties. Her left hand found the magic button and she indulged herself, the right finger matching time and motion as she molested her nipple.

Amanda had shifted the sculpture into position and parked the motorcycle out of the way. She waved the helmet into the target zone. The door was almost silent as it opened.

Amanda stood straddle-legged with her hands resting on her hips. As the door rolled up, she could see the bumper and then the lights and the hood. And then amusement washed her face as she watched the blonde having a violent orgasm in her car. It would have been funny, but Amanda found herself unsnapping her pants and shoving her right hand down to the satin panties that she had brought home and worn for the last two days. They were the ones Victoria had worn the day before and they were filled with her smell.

As Victoria regained her senses, her eyes fluttered open to focus on the figure in the doorway that was squirming and just as obvious in her orgasm as Victoria had probably been in hers. She waited and enjoyed the exhibition. Neither one had thought about the fact they could be seen from the street—or that not all cameras are obvious.

As Amanda finished and smiled sheepishly, she stepped aside and waved Victoria to pull the car in. As an afterthought, she pulled her right hand out of her pants but left the top snap undone. She raised her hand to her nose. The scent was a heady mix of Victoria and her. She licked her fingers and left the two middle ones in her mouth as her lover slowly rose from the car.

"I guess that takes the heat off the urgency."

Amanda walked over and Victoria gently pulled the hand out of her mouth and encased the fingers in her own—sucking. She moaned gently as her lips drew into a smile around the fingers.

Amanda removed her hand and replaced it with her mouth. Her hand returned to where it had been distracted before as the other hand cupped the other breast and rubbed the two hard nipples. The urgency was gone, but the sensation and enticing contact had their own effects. Soon, the pantyhose leg circled around the leather leg as the two women were pushed against the other.

The movements didn't reach the groping fevered pitch of before. This time, it was about just being together. The tongue wrestling became loving kissing and licking on necks and ears until they calmed and just stood serenely hanging on each other in a hug. Victoria drew in a deep breath that Amanda matched. They drew apart and Victoria took Amanda's hand.

Quietly, she asked, "Show me your home."

Amanda could see the afternoon sun was at the perfect light through the large windows high in the industrial space. Near the wall behind Victoria, Amanda had placed the large face sculpture. "Close your eyes and don't open them until I say."

She led her to the best place. The ridgeline almost burned with a golden fire. "Okay, open them."

The silence was deafening.

Victoria took one halting step forward.

"What do you think?" Amanda asked.

Victoria was silent. She opened her mouth, closed it, and then opened it again.

The lack of reaction roared loud in Amanda's ears. The one time she really put herself out there and there was… nothing. Time pulled out of space. She felt the panic rising from her gut into her throat. It was kissing Becky Feldman in tenth grade—all over again.

The same lack of reaction before the slap… the humiliation of her walking away. It was all starting over…

Victoria turned. Tears streamed down her face, her eyes awash. She could only make out a dark blur standing in front of her. She couldn't trust her legs to walk, so she just put out her arms and prayed. Her body shuddered with the silent crying, and then she succumbed to the anguished wail. It was every loss, every challenge, every slight, every missed birthday, every missed everything—all was healed in a single rush of overwhelming acceptance of the person she was. She recognized the lips of polished bronze—they were the same ones she saw in the mirror every morning. The pieced-together rough surface hinted at the foils in her life—and the lack of a smooth completeness. The empty eyes that allowed the viewer to glimpse the vastness of open possibilities... and it was created by the hands that she had come to love... and trust.

Their bodies enfolded and collapsed on the floor in a puddle. Neither cared about anything except the matching heartbeat and understanding. Two separate hearts—beating in a single joining. The sea of salty tears was licked and kissed away as their hunger to heal the other consumed them. No lust—but pure, accepting love. The two kissed until they couldn't breathe and then collapsed into each other's necks, panting.

"You'll get dirty down here."

"I don't care. This is where you are."

"I can be on the bed..."

Victoria glanced toward the bed. "Can I see your sculpture from there?"

"I'll move the bed."

The large room had long gone dark when Amanda had turned on a small spot lamp, pointed to wash across the large face. Victoria lay on her stomach in only her panties. Three of the pillows were under her chest and arms as she stared at the sculpture.

Between her spread legs, Amanda lay on her back with

her head pillowed on the satin-covered butt cheeks. Victoria lazily played with her nipples as she gently stroked her raised inner thighs. The evening had been intense and consuming, and they now drifted in the afterglow with thoughts only half formed.

"I want this pillow always." Amanda rolled over halfway and kissed the one cheek. Her hand clenched in between her own thighs. Her left hand slid along the smooth leg of her lover. The slight shiver of Victoria's skin was satisfying. She kneaded her head into the valley of satin between the two pads.

Amanda's feeling of satisfied calm, almost gave her permission to suck on her thumb like a child—she pulled her hand from her vagina and drew the two middle fingers in instead. The taste of Victoria's and her own juices still soaked the skin. She drifted.

"We only met a few weeks ago... How long did it take for you to do this?" Victoria was still amazed and excited by the face.

Amanda rolled over and buried her mouth and nose in the crevasse. She breathed in the scent deeply. There was no smell as powerful as recent sex. She languidly looked up at the large area of mixed metals and thought back. "I started cutting out the steel plates about six months ago."

Victoria thought about that information. She wiggled around until she was on her back and Amanda's head was in her crotch. Amanda took advantage of the position to plant a playful kiss. She knew that starting anything more that night was useless. She crawled up into her lover's arms and cuddled.

"So you planned this, but before you even knew me?"

Amanda nodded. "I was sick and had a fever. In the

night, I kept dreaming of this face with no eyes. When I looked into the eyes, I only saw the night sky. When the fever broke, it woke me up, and I penciled out what I remembered. I started cutting the steel a week later."

"Do you have what you sketched?"

"Sure." Amanda rolled over and got up. She pulled away the piece of paper taped to the wall. One of the corners tore off.

She handed it to Victoria. One glance and the older woman started laughing. "And this... is that?" The paper was filled with mathematical formulas.

Amanda giggled. "It is to me."

Victoria laughed even harder. "Well, I guess we know that nobody will ever steal your ideas."

Amanda took the paper and kissed Victoria deeply on the lips. Her secret was safe... and shared.

The two drifted in each other's arms while next door, Sam was working at a fevered pitch. His smile was a mix of lust and love for his adopted sister—and best friend.

Sam finally finished the video he had been working on all evening. It had been a gift of fate—his walking by the large monitor screens that afternoon. They showed the feed from his new high-resolution security cameras. Seven of the eight cameras in Amanda's alley entrance had been active and recording in high definition color. The cameras themselves looked like just a brick out of place or a fat brick. To the casual observer, they were invisible as part of the wall. They would become his next great patent and product.

Sam took all of the feeds of the two women masturbating and turned them into a montage that had their solo performances appearing as if they were entertaining each other. He boiled the longer clip down to three minutes and then downgraded it to play on a phone. He saved a copy and sent it.

His sister, Jody, was going to love the preview.

He would send the larger file through the file sharing cloud he shared with her—later. He leaned back as he stared at the blown up freeze frame of Amanda's face. He smiled softly. *It was good to finally see her so happy.*

19

IN MANY WAYS, the week had flown by. The meeting on Monday established many new areas that the law firm had wanted, as well as some of the new equipment that they needed.

On Tuesday, Amanda went over much of the software that they were using with the three IT people who were on staff. She hadn't been completely enamored with two of them, but she bit her tongue. Replacing them with superior tech geeks would be a delicate process for down the road.

Wednesday morning had the new equipment arrive, and the day went from an easy ten hours to well into the night. On Thursday morning, Amanda dragged herself up to Victoria's penthouse and fell into bed next to Victoria's sleeping body. She thought about kissing the cheek good night but never made it—both were exhausted from the long hours.

"OKAY, LIGHT HER up." Amanda stood and her eyes danced from light to light. She knew exactly which ones should be on and which should be blinking.

The young blond with the long hair and red Vans sneakers stood next to her. Amanda almost sensed that he was breathing rapidly—almost panting. "Are you okay?"

He turned with a quirky smile. "Come on—tell me this shit doesn't give you a hard... on..." His voice faded. Red rose out of his black Teenage Mutant Ninja Turtle T-shirt.

Amanda gave him a deadpan look. She knew exactly what he was talking about. She looked down at the two very hard nipples pushing against her dirty white tank top. She noticed that there were three holes in this one... *but who gave a fuck.* She leaned forward and looked at the guy's crotch. She stood up and gave him a smile. "I see your one and raise you one."

"Yeah, you win." They fist bumped and turned back to the four large racks. "So, do you think this will hold them for a while?" He was referring to the huge capacity of storage that they had also installed.

"Not hardly. They're getting a contract that right now is stored on twenty old Crays. The company they're taking over doesn't have the wherewithal to grow in size or storage. There will be a whole new room next month down in the sub-basement, and we'll have to start building out a space that's about ten times this."

She turned to the other geek. "Hopefully, that'll take them down the road for at least a few years while we figure out where to take it all off-site and still maintain the level of security. But if they take on any more federal jobs, they'll have to rent space in Yucca Mountain." Amanda's eyes kept assessing the flow of tattletale lights. She had enjoyed working with another high-level geek.

They turned at the knock on the door. Amanda called

out, "We're back here."

She heard Paul's voice. "Exactly where *is* back here?"

"Keep to your right and head toward the back of the computers."

He came around the corner. He looked as if the day hadn't had any effect on him. Either that, or he had just put on a fresh black suit, shirt, and tie.

Amanda held out her arms and hands at the new computer towers that were even taller than the man in the suit. "Welcome to your new world, Paul."

He watched the twinkling and changing lights on the black expanse. He could see large ropes of wires that came together, ran for a while, and then split off again. None of it made any sense to him.

"But will this paper airplane make it through a window across the street?"

Amanda smiled at his reference to their conversation that felt so very long ago. "And hit the jerk at the conference table that is texting instead of paying attention."

He smiled at Amanda. "It's very impressive. But then, so is your motorcycle and everything else mechanical that baffles me."

"I told you, Paul… anytime you want to hop on the back, I'll take you for a ride."

He smirked. "I'll take a pass and save us both the embarrassing image of me crouched like a large spider on your back."

Amanda understood. "So what can we do you for?"

"Can we talk?" He looked at the geek.

Amanda's eyebrow rose as she side glanced at the blonde tech. "Excuse me. I need to… um…" and the young man was gone.

Paul watched him leave. Turning, he wasn't sure what to say. He had come to talk to Amanda, and he was used to her unusual attire… He was uncomfortable with himself that he didn't realize there was anyone who worked for him—who wasn't dressed in business attire. He now found himself on unstable ground. "How… um, he…?"

"He's the best you have. You can fire the other two at the end of the day and never skip a beat. What you need are two more like Danny. If you want, I'll troll the gutters and alleys."

Paul blinked. He hadn't expected the brash appraisal, but then he was still getting used to Amanda. "I need your pass card."

"Because I gave you my honest opinion of Danny or because I was honest about the other two?"

"All of the above…and everything else." He held out his hand, flapping his fingers.

Amanda frowned but fished the card out of her back pocket. She handed him the white card.

He held it up. "This one got you in the front door of the building and to enter the offices during business hours. It also let you come to the penthouse level and Victoria's apartment." Amanda nodded.

He held up a black card in his other hand. "This one allows you full access to the building, the offices, as well as Victoria's and my apartments. I understand we are starting new construction on a room like this one in the lower basement. When it's time, we will code its access off your card. You will be the master access. It seemed the most fitting." He leaned over and kissed her lightly on the cheek as he handed her the card. Tenderly, his voice cracked. "Welcome to our little family. And thank you for hearing Victoria out when it was important."

He stood upright, looking down at the young woman. Her lips were curled in tight between her teeth. She slowly looked up with tears in her eyes. "I don't know what to say. Hell, I don't know where to go with what I'm feeling right now." She gave up, buried her face in his chest, and cried as she hugged him.

He hesitated, and then finally draped his arms around her softly.

As Amanda caught her breath, she stepped back, wiping away snot with the back of her hand. As she also wiped her eyes to clear them, she noticed he was holding a handkerchief. They shrugged and laughed.

He put it back in his pocket. "Well… you know… just in case."

Amanda smirked kindly. "Yeah… I'll know where it is next time."

He looked at the computer again. "It really is impressive. I mean, I was impressed with what you did with my phone, but this is amazing. When I asked Danny this morning if we really needed all of this, he told me all about what it will do for us—and that this all came out of your mind—not our IT department." He turned and rested his hand on her shoulder. "He also told me the same thing about the other two. Only he said that once you started explaining the new technology, the other two were lost. They were gone at lunch."

He jerked and reached into his shirt pocket and pulled out another black card. This one was a credit card. "Victoria is taking you shopping this evening. Don't let her use her card. She'll use her personal, and I think the partners would rather say thank you for all of your help." He handed her the card.

Amanda stared at it. It was a corporate credit card—with her name on it. She looked up. He was smiling. "Like I said… welcome to the family."

"Do I work here?"

He thought a moment. "Whether you live here is between you two. Whether you work here is entirely up to you. You do seem to relate to Danny…"

She smiled a quirky grin. "Ah, he's just part of the geeky nerd family."

There was a soft knock on the door.

Paul smiled. "We're back here."

"Oh, you are fucking kidding me. I am not going near that monster… I've seen that space movie."

They laughed and Amanda took one last glancing run through on the lights and connections. "Tomorrow, if it hasn't raped any children, burned down the school, or run off with an STD spreader, we'll start the integration process. But I want a two-week burn-in period before we get them married."

They walked around the computer to find Victoria waiting with her purse.

Paul had joined them for dinner at a nice little bistro on 21st. At the mention of shopping for clothes, Paul bowed out and Amanda wanted to just run. Victoria held her close and whispered in her ear, *"There are rewards afterward."* Amanda behaved.

Most of the items they set up for deliverey the next morning at the penthouse. Dutifully, Amanda whipped out the black card and showed it to Victoria before presenting it to the sales clerk. Amanda was afraid that Victoria was going to molest her there in the shop, but it was a restrained hug. The two smiled knowingly.

The last few packages, they carried out and put in the car. As they got in, Amanda looked at Victoria. "Are you sure about this? I mean, you don't have to go—"

"Who was on the phone last week that I cut off?"

Amanda giggled. "Jody."

Victoria's head snapped around. Her face was pure terror. "Jody… as in, *'Thank you, Jody?'*"

Amanda nodded with a smirk. "The one and only."

"Oh, fuck."

"Maybe not."

Victoria frowned. "Wait, what does she have to do with your twin's wedding?"

"It's her show. It's what she does… wedding planning."

"Oh, crap. And I told her how to do her business."

"Isn't that your expertise? Telling businesses what to do?"

"That's different."

"Look, how about we drive and get this past Paul first."

Later, Amanda stood in front of the mirror and ran her fingers through her hair. Then she scrunched and pulled, and finally shook her hair out like a wet dog. She laughed at the woman in the mirror. With a few little pulls here and there, it once again fell into place just as Freddie said it would. *The man is a fucking genius.*

She turned and opened the bathroom door. The marble floor felt cool and wonderful on her bare feet. She walked into the living area and struck a pose with her one hand tipped into the leather pants pocket with the other resting back on her ass. Her torso was turned and the soft pearl-pink silk blouse had just enough body-conscious fit to hug her breasts. The nipples were very evident. The black leather pants were a body-conscious version of a standard Western boot cut jean.

Victoria sat stunned. She tried to speak and yet was speechless. She slowly rose and carefully made her way over, as if she were afraid to move rapidly or to say anything that would turn the vision into a dissipating mirage. She walked around Amanda. Everything was as she had imagined, and yet the sum total was more. There was a nice touch of soft femininity with just enough of the hard tomboy body to show through.

"If you don't talk, I'll have to throw on a tank top and leave."

"I'm stunned. You were always you… but now you're… I don't know how to say it without it coming out as an insult or backhanded compliment. Now you're beautifully you." She stopped in front of Amanda. She stood with a face of worry and uncertainty. "Did that sound wrong?"

Amanda thought about it. "What you meant to say is that I clean up nice?"

Victoria rushed into a hug. "Oh, gawd. Now who's the person with words?"

"Let's go see what kind of words Paul has."

They stopped at the door on the way out. Victoria pushed the bottom button. "Paul, do you have a few minutes?"

A moment later, the deep voice flowed from the intercom. "Sure. There or here?"

"We're on our way."

They opened the door and stepped out into the small hallway as Paul opened his door. He stood in the door and then his eyes lit up. "Vicky, are you dating a new stud?"

"We need your opinion."

"Well, the first thing that comes to my mind is your new favorite word—fuck."

Victoria laughed. "No, she's taken. But you're always welcome to a hug."

Amanda struck her pose. "Any other thoughts, big guy?"

He frowned. "Yeah, there *is* one thought… will your knives fit under those new leather pants? I mean, those tight boots would ruin the line of the pants."

Amanda broke her pose. "They'd fit, but I'd never be able to pull them out. They're just too long."

"Where she's wearing this outfit doesn't require knives, swords, or guns. Well, other than a single knife to cut the wedding cake."

Paul smiled and nodded in final understanding. "Hence the slight blush of pink to the shirt."

Amanda chuckled. "Smart boy… got it in one."

"Well, then, maybe you two should come in. I put a bottle of champagne on ice about an hour ago."

Amanda's mouth opened in question.

Victoria leaned over, and in a stage whisper, she divulged. "Don't buy any of his bullshit. He has three bottles of Dom lying in his fridge at all times. Remember, he *is* a lawyer. He lies for a living."

20

THE DAY HAD started out a bit late, as Amanda put in a call the night before and got an early emergency meeting. With Victoria's approval, they sped out of town just ahead of the morning rush of traffic. Even then, the traffic of the I-5 was against them. The main problem with Oregon traffic was the two seasons—accidents from rain and construction.

While they waited out a long line through some major work on an area that had flooded out the previous winter, Amanda took advantage of the stop to unbuckle and roll back and recline her seat.

"What are you doing?" Victoria frowned. "Don't you dare go to sleep on me."

Amanda rolled over and ran her hand in the cowl neck of the soft cashmere sleeveless sweater. She was happy to feel that Victoria had chosen a chemise over a bra. The nipple rose to meet her hand as Victoria's mouth opened to accept the incoming tongue and lips.

The kiss was brief and then Amanda rolled back and shucked out of her boots and motorcycle pants. She smiled at Victoria.

"You are *not* going to ride down the highway in just your panties." Although she was also taking special delight in seeing the new red lace boy pants. Amanda had admitted they were more comfortable than the thong, but she wasn't giving up her thongs just yet.

Amanda rolled up her leather motorcycle pants around her boots and knives. She tossed them on the back seat as she reached for the large bag in the footwell behind her. Reaching into the bag, she pulled out the weathered cowgirl-cut jeans and slid them on. They were not lined like her leathers, but they felt similar.

From the bag, she took out her new low-rise boots. She checked the new system out and pulled them on. The cuffs of the jeans fit over the boots perfectly. She made a few adjustments and was satisfied. It had been years since she had worn any denim, but the weathered softness was close to what she liked on her skin.

"What do you think?"

Victoria smiled as the line of cars started to finally move forward. "Actually, I liked the panty idea better, but we would never have made it halfway down the state. Do they work?"

"The man is a genius. And to think he was already making them for me…"

"So, the best of both worlds." She smiled over at Amanda.

"Office attire." They laughed.

The miles rolled by, between the herds of orange pylons. Even with making great time, they finally stopped for the day when they reached Shasta. The motel was clean, and when the guy said all he had available were two queens, they just nodded tiredly. The room was clean and, most importantly, the window faced east for the early morning sun.

"Dinner?" The question was more of a comment about energy than a consideration of meal.

The clerk had suggested the small café bar when Amanda asked about a good steak. The place was quiet, and the three old men at the bar reminded them both of Jeff's bar. For Amanda, it felt like home.

The steak dinners arrived, and at first, Victoria thought Amanda had fainted or was doing something weird like smelling the beef. But when she leaned back, she had a large smile drawn to one side.

"Japanese or Sarisan?"

Victoria looked at her and furrowed her brow. "What are you…?"

"How do you want to cut your meat? Japanese Samurai or Damascus Scimitar?" She held up her two new blades. Both blades were almost two inches or so wide and only the length of her finger. The handles fit in her palms perfectly. Tim had taken many casts of Amanda's hands when he made her other knives. These he had incorporated into a pair of more dress-style boots. The handles and blades were hiding in plain sight and provided easy access. Victoria could tell by the look on her lover's face—the woman was in love with her new toys.

"Your choice."

Through the meal, the two knives rested on the plates between them. They each tried out the two blades and how they cut. Victoria was more fascinated by the unusual handles with the large hole in the end, large enough to put her thumb through.

"Can you tell any difference in how they cut?"

Amanda chewed as she nodded. She took a sip of her wine and wiped at her mouth.

"Sure, but it has nothing to do with how the blade is made. It is all in how the edge is created. The katana blade is ground only on the one side—the same as a sushi knife is. This provides a stronger edge without the fine angle. Over the long run, it would hold its sharp edge longer than the Damascus.

"But the beauty for the eye is in how the Damascus is made. The many layers of the two steels are revealed with the acid etch that darkens the higher carbon layer. Although it's basically a weaker design and dulls faster, the beauty is in the long, slow taper of the blade. The grind is actually that fine reflective part that runs along the edge." She held the knife up to the candlelight.

"That line looks like what you did with the edge of the upper lip on the sculpture… which I love, if I didn't tell you before." They both smiled at the many times she had told her.

"All three lines cut deep."

"Three?"

"That fine line is also along your upper lip as well… which I love, if I didn't tell you before."

"If I weren't so tired, I'd make you explain that part again." She smiled wanly at the brunette.

"It has been a very long week."

Victoria cut the last piece of her meat and was examining the knife handle. She had her ring finger half inserted in the hole. "I don't get the hole."

Amanda wasn't sure she should explain… but then decided there would be no judgment. The woman knew about the knives and their constant part of Amanda's life.

"In a knife fight, the last thing you want—is to lose possession of your knife. The hole not only makes it a more secure grip but also provides several options of how to hold the knife."

"But these are very small knives. Surely, you wouldn't bring these to a knife fight? Wouldn't you want to use your big ones?"

"Normally, on a dark night on Southeast 10th, sure—but not because of what you think. The size and that they are standing out on my boots would keep most punks away. The one who would try me would also be the stupid one. So the length with a loft hold would be the preferred knife and fighting stance." She lightly bounced the handle in her open hand with the blade pointed forward.

"But if the action is in a tighter area, like an elevator or small bar like this one, these are the ones to go to."

"But the size?"

"A small blade only an inch long can still kill someone just as fast as or faster than a large blade. More important is stopping the fight before any real damage is done." She flipped the knife around in one blurring move and showed the knife sticking out of the outside of her fist. "This way, I can hit or swing through and slice open something very bloody like a forehead. The amount of blood that can spill from a deep cut across the forehead can blind someone and stops the fight with only a dozen stitches or so."

Victoria looked at the fist, the knife, and the woman she had only known for a very short time. But now, she couldn't imagine her life without her. Even though, she realized, she knew so very little about her.

Victoria put down her fork and patted carefully at her mouth. The entire time, she held Amanda's eyes with hers.

"If someone attacked me, would you defend me?"

"Yes."

"With your life?" The question was the ultimate question that anyone could ask of another—*would you lay down your life for me?*

Amanda leaned the knife on her plate. "I understand what you're asking, even if you don't really understand what it all means—but the answer is an emphatical yes."

Victoria leaned back almost as if she had been slapped. The power of the answer was soul-shaking in its raw honesty and meaning.

Amanda reached out her hand, and only their fingertips touched.

"In that event, it's not like taking a bullet for the President of the United States. When it comes to hand to hand combat, once you have engaged a person whose intentions are bodily harm or death, you may have started by defending someone, but the second you engage, it's about your own survival. So what sounds altruistic, and may well be, is not as pure in the practice as the saying."

Victoria's voice was little more than a whisper. "But to even have the inner certainty… to voice that level of conviction…"

"To know that I love you enough?"

"Yes."

"Would you defend me in court if I had to kill that person?"

"Of course, I would. We would throw the entire firm at it and hire the best legal team in the country…"

Amanda took back up her knife and held it up. "We each fight with the weapons we are best with. Mine are the sword and computers. Yours are your knowledge and mind.

I'm not sure which is deadlier, but I know I can trust that you'll always have my back. I think I knew it when you took that first sip of a bad beer and were almost willing to take another sip just to be with me."

"But you got me a better beer."

"You were worth it."

Something was stinging at Victoria's eyes. She quickly grabbed her purse, pulled out several bills and put them on the table. Her voice was cracking, "We need to leave now." She noticed both knives were missing from the table as Amanda pushed her chair back.

21

THE SUNRISE FOUND them thrown across only one of the beds. The soft little kisses turned to slow tender ones, but not much more than cuddling and snuggling. The night had consumed the last of a small fire that smoldered. The fire that now burned was more of the candle of the truth of their relationship.

A little bit of grab-ass prevailed between the curtain that separated the toilet and the small tub.

Victoria rinsed her hair and wound it tight to wring it out. "Remind me when we get home I need to get my shower remodeled; not as big as yours—but big enough for those little stools. After all, we can't get your motorcycle in the elevator."

Amanda laughed. "Obviously, you've never ridden in the freight elevator of your building."

The curtain swept back and Victoria's head stuck out. "Really? It would fit?" Her eyes twinkled like a kid at Christmas and Amanda laughed.

"How do you think they got that big ass grand piano into Paul's apartment?"

"He doesn't have a piano in his apartment..."

Amanda shrugged. "With hands like that..."

The remaining drive was pleasant and open. The air conditioner mitigated the California heat, and they finally pulled off the freeway. As Amanda drove the familiar way up into the Piedmont Hills behind Berkeley, Victoria ogled the lush scenery. "This is beautiful..."

Amanda shrugged. "I like Portland better."

"But you grew up here."

"Don't get me wrong, it had its perks. But it's also where I grew up. I chose to move to Portland even though the Silicon Valley is just across the bridge, a left turn, and down about twenty miles on the right. Speaking of which..." They pulled up and parked at the green house.

As they walked up the driveway, Victoria looked around the neighborhood. It reminded her of her parent's choice to live after she had moved out. Three-thousand miles away, and her parent's street could have been the next street over—but in Boston.

Amanda rang the bell.

"You ring the bell at your parent's house?"

"The house I grew up in was about seven blocks and lifetime from here."

The door flew open and a brunette dressed in an over-sized plaid flannel shirt and white shorts stood tossing her long mane of hair. "Manly!" she shouted. She grabbed Amanda's hand and jerked her into a huge hug and deep tongue-drenched kiss as her hand sought the ass cheek that her one leg was hooked around.

Victoria stood shocked... but enthralled. Maybe even a little turned on. Okay, maybe a lot.

Suddenly, the tall, muscular woman pulled a laughing Amanda out of the way and fixed her eyes on Victoria. "Yum. You are even better in real life. Look at those tits. No wonder Manly was doing a standing orgasm. They're bigger than mine." She reached out and pulled Victoria into her arms and mouth as the one leg hooked behind Victoria's linen slacks and rode up and down as their two crotches ground into each other.

Despite being accosted by an unknown woman, Victoria was also very aroused.

Everything changed as Victoria felt a reassuring hand of Amanda's on the space between her shoulder blades. With gentle pressure, she felt herself relaxing into the other woman's breasts—which she was sure were almost as large.

Amanda's breath was almost panting, as well as hot in her ear. "Now is the time to say, '*Thank you, Jody.*'"

This realization was the release Victoria needed as the consuming heat in her groin and the grinding on her clit sent spasm after spasm through her as Jody joined her in a dry-hump orgasm. Amanda draped her arms over the two and kissed their cheeks and ears—anything she could find available.

Jody regained her breath. "Welcome to the family. I've seen so much about you."

"Seen?" Amanda and Victoria frowned as one.

Jody laughed. "Sam sent me some security video of you two playing at Manly's. It was so hot I've almost rubbed myself raw."

Amanda pulled back a bit. "He got those flat feeds to finally work?"

Jody nodded with a laugh. "Good enough to see you two going at it in vivid clarity."

"I want to see it."

Victoria growled with a smile. "So do I."

Jody laughed. "Only if you still have those shiny panties on… those were hot… and that silk blouse without a bra—wow." She took a step and giggled. "Let's see if I can walk first."

The three hung on each other and stumbled into the house laughing. As they neared the closed double doors, they could hear violin music playing.

Jody opened the door and the music stopped. The young blond turned. Except for the mustache and the hair color, Victoria was staring at a mirror image of Amanda.

"Manly." The man tenderly laid down the violin in its case. "And that would mean this is the Victoria Jody has told me so much about." He extended his hand and they shook.

The hand was as different from Amanda's as Victoria was from Amanda. The hand was long and slender, almost delicate, but with a steel strength that Victoria could feel. "So you must be the Twat Twin."

"Nope, I *am* her twin… but it's just Twat. You can call me Allen if you want."

"So, Allen, now that I've finally met you, my assumption that you were a female is dashed."

Jody laughed. "Because Twat is a dude?"

Victoria nodded.

"It's the same reason they call me Manly," Amanda explained. "When we were in high school, there was an asshole named Timmy Winter. He was the captain of the football team and the darling of the coaches and cheer squad and everyone else he could fool. Ever since we were young, he was a bully. In high school, he figured out what the dick between his legs was for. He turned it on the girls—and he didn't take no for an answer.

"He knocked up a couple of the cheerleaders, but that got hushed up, and they went to visit relatives for a while. But then he raped a girl that I was getting to know, and love. It didn't matter that she would never be mine permanently… but she told him no and he wouldn't listen. When she told me, I was pissed." Victoria could see that it still affected Amanda.

Jody softly hugged Amanda's arm and laid her head on Amanda's shoulder. Victoria finally understood their relationship.

Allen continued the story. "When she came looking for Tim, he was busy with his monthly beating of me. Something he had been doing since the fifth grade. She came around the corner of the gym, Tim was bent over me and going to town with his fist. Manly took one look, dropkicked his nuts all the way to the top of his head and rang the bell. As he turned, she didn't realize she'd knocked him out already, and she round-housed him and shattered his jaw."

Amanda laughed through her clenched teeth. "It broke six of the bones in my hand, but it felt so fucking good that I didn't stop there."

Allen grabbed at Amanda's arm to hold himself up as he laughed. "He bounced on the grass, and she started working him over with the big ass steeltoed engineer boots she used to wear."

Jody laughed. "We had to pull her off when the paramedics arrived. The teachers couldn't get to them. All of the girls made a wall around the fight and egged Manly on."

"I broke about half of his ribs and his jaw. I'm not sure either of his nuts survived the trip north."

Allen finished. "While Tim was in the hospital, his

folks sold their house. Nobody knows where they moved to, but the jerk was never seen again."

"But where do the names Manly and Twat come from?"

Amanda laughed. "You heard what he does for a living… he plays the violin like a little girl."

Jody shrugged. "And Manly wore… well… manly clothes. She always wore jeans, boots, and work shirts. The girl's dean told her she had to wear dresses and she told the old biddy to take her tight sweaters and shove them up her cunt until the itch stopped."

"So if I was the manly one of the twins, then Twat was the twat."

Victoria shook her head. "I just find it… well… confusing."

Amanda reached around and hugged Victoria. "So how can we make it okay for you?"

Victoria leaned her head on Amanda's. "I don't know. How about Mandi?

Allen laughed and pulled on her arm. "Oh, please, Mandi, pretty please? Can you be Mandi, and I can just be Allen? The other day at practice…"

Jody shrieked with laughter. "I slipped and called him Twat."

He lowered his head and looked through the tops of his eyes. "In front of the conductor."

The four laughed.

Amanda finally controlled herself. "Fuck you, Twat. You need to grow a pair and be Al."

Jody smiled. "I can live with that… Al and Mandi. Yup, works for me." She leaned in and kissed him hotly. "Mmm, yeah, I like the feel of big Al. Maybe if you play your cards right, I'll let you be on top tomorrow night." The man smiled.

He looked at his watch and begged out about picking up his tux. He kissed Victoria's cheek sweetly and left.

Jody slumped. "God! I thought we would never get rid of him." She stepped over to the giant wall-mounted TV, plugged in her phone and toggled to the high-definition version of the movie. "Amanda, close the door and lock it. Ladies, it's time to drop your pants because this is hot!"

In sixty-three glorious inches of living color, the split screen showed Victoria in her car on the left and Amanda standing in the roll-up doorway on the right. Both were busy in their pants.

Soon, three other hands were busy in three other pants.

"Play it again." Victoria giggled. Nothing had seemed so dirty… and so right, in her life.

As they finally just laid there watching the video for the umpteenth time, Jody softly played with Victoria's nipple as she draped naked across the other two. Amanda leaned over against Jody's other arm and her hand had long come to a stop playing among Victoria's legs and pussy.

"So, before you cut me off the other day, you said you had both sides of the wedding party covered. How?"

Victoria smiled softly. "Your only criterion was that it had to have a pink blush."

"Correct. My dress is pink."

Victoria rolled her head. "Wait… What? You're marrying Twat?"

"Of course, who did you think…?"

"I didn't know."

Amanda mumbled sleepily. "I only told her that you were the wedding planner."

Jody squealed with laughter.

"So what did you come up with?" She turned toward Amanda. "I'm dying to see what kind of dress *you* came up with."

Victoria rolled her head back down and snuggled firmer in the other woman's lap. "It's a loose A-line, kind of like a Donna Reed look that hits just below the knee. I'll be wearing matching low pumps with it and a discreet string of pink freshwater pearls."

Amanda chuckled. "I'll be wearing black leather tuxedo pants and boots with a silk charmeuse-satin tux shirt with the placards running matte and shiny. It has double French cuffs, and it is a soft mother of pearl pink. I'll be on the Twat's side."

Jody laughed. *Welcome to the crazy wonderful family.*

22

THE MAN SLOWLY walked around the sculpture. His thin briefcase hung from his left hand. The receptionist watched as the man seemed more awestruck by the sculpture than most clients did. She could tell there was not one small detail that escaped the eyes of this balding middle-aged man in the tweed suit.

"Sir, is there something I can help you with?"

The man twitched but seemed only slightly distracted.

"Sir?"

He turned, but his right arm and finger were still pointing at the face as if magnetically drawn to it. "Yes. I… um… I think I have an appointment with… with that."

"The sculpture?"

"Yes. I mean, no." He glanced back at the metal face. "I mean that face… Oh, heavens. That's… I mean that person." The man was a complete bumbling idiot or the sculpture had unhinged him.

The receptionist looked at her monitor for appointments. "Are you Mr. Messinheimer?"

"Lloyd, yes, Lloyd Messinheimer."

"You have an appointment with Ms. Dumas."

"Yes." He sounded unsure. "I suppose I do."

"If you care to take a seat, Karen will be right out to get you."

The man distractedly pointed at the face. "Can I? I mean…"

The receptionist resisted the urge to roll her eyes. She supposed she was starting to get used to the reaction of many of the clients. She held out her hand toward the sculpture.

The man stepped back over as if it were a guilty pleasure.

A few minutes later, Karen walked into the lobby to find only the two receptionists. She frowned at not finding a client. She looked to the two receptionists, who moved as twins. They rolled their eyes and nodded at the sculpture.

Karen saw that the face had sprouted legs.

"Mr. Messinheimer?"

A head poked out around the metal sculpture. "Yes… yes, that would be me."

He walked around the sculpture as if he were magnetically attracted, barely able to achieve escape velocity. He stumbled and looked back as he reached Karen. He turned and leaned in toward her.

"Extraordinary piece, simply extraordinary…"

"Yes, I agree. How was your trip down from Seattle?"

"Seattle?"

"Didn't you just come from Seattle?" She guided him down the hallway with the secretarial pool on the left and conference rooms on the other.

"I had a connection through… oh, yes, I guess it was Seattle. But I'm here from New York."

Karen stopped and turned as she held out her left arm and hand. "Ah, yes, my mistake, New York. Can I get you anything to drink? Coffee, tea, soda?"

"No, I'm fine, thank you."

"Ms. Dumas is just finishing up and will be only a few minutes. Make yourself comfortable."

The young woman in the white blouse and black satin slacks excused herself as she slid around Karen into the conference room. She nodded to Karen, and they both twitched a tiny smile. Her hands and fingers were deft as the young woman worked on the small notepad. The windows darkened to a medium-dark warm gray as a video began to play on the one wall. She watched for a moment, and then closed the door behind her as she noticed the man sitting down, already mesmerized by the images of metal flowing upon the wall. Amanda ran her right hand through her hair, touched a few more places on the pad, and smiled as the glass wall between her in the hallway and the man at the table darkened. She never tired of playing with the Bat Cave toys she had installed that subtly set this firm apart from any other firm their clients had ever dealt with.

Victoria walked down the hallway, her closed smile pulled to one side. Her eyes twinkled—this was the big day. She watched Amanda standing, watching the video of her metalwork through the only glass that would not darken or become opaque—the door. Victoria stopped at her side. Putting her arm around Mandi's waist, she leaned her wash of blonde curls over the brunette's shoulder as she rested head on head and then turned and kissed her cheek. Everything she could say had already been said a hundred times. She felt the steel in Amanda's stance, but the nervous vibrating was now calm. Victoria and Amanda watched the video to the end, standing with their arms openly around each other. The forty people in the secretarial pool came and went without much more than a glance. The three years since that afternoon on the sidewalk outside the bar felt like a lifetime—and yet as sudden as last week.

As the video ended, Victoria turned her head and whispered. "Have I told you this morning how much I love you?"

Amanda chuckled softly. "Only six times. You're slipping, but who's counting." She smiled and turned. "I don't have time for all your lawyer bullshit. Just fucking give me a hug."

The hug was short but complete. As Victoria turned, she muttered, "Give me ten minutes and then bring in the Spider."

The clock in Amanda's mind started the countdown as she watched Victoria open the glass door. "Good morning, Mr. Messinheimer. I am Victoria Dumas. It's an honor for you to come all this..." The sound-deadening glass door closed on the rest of her opening argument.

At nine minutes and fifty-eight seconds, Amanda wound up the sculpture that they had named *The Spider*. She hid it in her palm and quietly entered the room. Amanda received only a distracted glance. She sat down at the head of the long table and placed her two hands in a protective igloo over the sculpture. Then she let it go.

The twelve legs started walking. The movement was a cross between an arachnid and a starfish. The body was a mix of a scarab and a head of a lion. The mane was darkened bronze, the face polished brass. The legs were copper, as was the heat-treated body.

The man glanced, distracted, at the quietly approaching sculpture when it was only about half the distance. He returned to the conversation; but had forgotten the question that Victoria had asked.

The man frowned. "I'm sorry, but what was the question again?" His head snapped back around. "What's that?"

Victoria did not answer as she let the man watch the kinetic sculpture play out. They had spent many nights playing with the Spider to make it move just the right way and distance. The seat the man had sat in had been the only seat pulled out or that had wheels that would roll. He had been guided as a lamb to slaughter—and just as innocent.

The Spider reached the spot directly in front of the man. It stopped, shuttered and turned. The long legs retracted into the carapace, and the sculpture lay on the table with its back end facing the man. Suddenly, the wings snapped open and fluttered as a laser light shimmered back and forth from inside the body. In the fan of laser light, two words appeared in the ethereal light.

"Hello, Lloyd."

The man, stunned, began to clap. "Bravo, bravo."

He looked to Amanda. "Excellent presentation of a kinetic art piece. Is it a Ruddy, as well?" His face snapped back and forth from Amanda and Victoria. He settled on Victoria. "Well, is it a Ruddy?"

Victoria offered her hand toward the end of the table and Amanda. "I think it would be best if you asked Amanda Ruddy herself."

The man at first frowned at Victoria. His brain was not taking in the information and finding a place for it to fit in his beliefs about whom the artist must be. Then he looked at Amanda, and as she nodded, his mouth fell open ever so slightly.

Amanda looked at her partner. Victoria nodded.

Amanda leaned forward, clasped her hands, and smiled warmly. "Mr. Messinheimer, I believe there's a price on the table for the rights to travel the show. Are the terms agreeable to you?"

"You… You're A. Ruddy?"

Amanda stood. "I am. Ms. Dumas is my attorney and representative. The offer on the table is fair and equitable. In five seconds, I will walk out that door taking the offer with me. It will never be offered to your museum again. It's time to commit or lose." She turned toward the door.

"No, wait! I mean… well, there are…"

Amanda put her hand on the doorknob as the Spider made one last twitch of mechanical life. All of the legs and wings snapped closed with a final metallic sound like a lock turning. The sculpture was now just a solid metal hemisphere. The sound startled the nervous man.

"Yes!"

Amanda smiled, opened the door, and as she stepped into the doorway, she nodded. "You'll never regret your decision Mr. Messinheimer." She closed the door behind her and walked down the hall.

She had just become a millionaire in her own right, doing something she loved, with a woman she loved just as much. She needed to go Skype Jody and Al and make disgusting auntie noises at her twin nieces.